MW00666918

EX LIBRIS

Paper Girls

ROOOO
Pape

Girls

BOOK THREE

writer
BRIAN K. VAUGHAN

artist
CLIFF CHIANG

colors
MATT WILSON

letters
JARED K. FLETCHER

IMAGECOMICS.COM

Dee Cunniffe - Color Flats
Jared K. Fletcher - Logo + Book Design

PAPER GIRLS DELUXE EDITION, BOOK 3. November 2020. Published by Image Comics, Inc. Office of publication: 2701 NW Vaughn St., Suite 780, Portland, OR 97210. Printed in China. For international rights, contact: foreignlicensing@imagecomics.com

ISBN: 978-1-5343-1648-5

CHAPTER 21

READING IS RAD
NEXT!
Circulation
Hey.
So, if I have my own card, can I check out, like, *any* book?
Let me guess.
Flowers in the Attic?
PUBLIC LIBRARY

What's *Flowers in the--*
Forget I even said it.
How old are you, Miss Coyle?
Twelve.
Essentially.
And what, you want the new Stephen King door-stopper? Because it's checked out, all three copies.
Nah, my brother tried to get me to read that green one...*Eyes of the Dragon,* but I'm not really into fantasy shit.
Sorry, fantasy **crap.**
Kid, if you're holding anything shy of *The Anarchist's Cookbook,* I'm going to be severely disappointed.
FRANCINE PASCAL
SWEET VALLEY HI
2
What Jessica wants, Jessica gets— even if someone gets hurt!
SECRETS
created by
PASCAL

Hmm.
I'm not in high school.
You don't say.
Everyone in my class is still obsessed with *Baby-Sitters Club*, but I think ***they're*** a bunch of babies.
RAD
Anyway, this book just looks...more interesting.
Well, it's the deep end of the pool, all right.
But, I think you can handle it.
For real?
Just get it back ***on time.***
You're going to be dying of leukemia any day now.

Oh.
I almost forgot.
We never do.
Did you really think you could ***escape?***
Into some book?
Only dorks want to escape life.

Hold it.
I don't play field hockey.
THEN I GUESS WE DO
What does that even--
Mac.
Muh?
Mac, get up.

We gotta keep moving.

I thought we were gonna wait until dawn.
That's exactly what Erin and I still think.
But KJ and Double-Oh Tiff say we should stay put.
That's what we're calling you now?
Only because "Tiffany 2000" sounds like a bad Cinemax sex robot.
Whatever, the only grownup here agrees with me.
We should clear out before the dicks on dinosaurs realize there were *people* inside that thing.

I'm sure the old-timers have been looking for the five of us this whole time.
Hell, a few of those things have passed right overhead!
But they haven't spotted us because we're pretty much *invisible* to people from the future.
Says who, Erin?
Well, *uhm,* that's what my... my *clone* said.
My evil clone.
Exactly.
And if all that stuff about their sensors being blind to our DNA or whatever was a lie, then we're sitting ducks out here.
So we just leave? We have no idea where we *are*. We don't even know what *year* we crashed into!
Enough.
If I'm the tiebreaker, I vote with Kaje's team.
We've got a perfectly good hiding spot and you want to charge into unknown territory?
It's not unknown...

...I think it might be *downtown.*
Is that the Terminal Tower?
I know, I remember it looking bigger back in '88.
But unless they gifted it to another city like a much-shittier Statue of Liberty, this is still *Cleveland.*
Come on.
The nearest branch isn't far from here.
Nearest branch of *what?*
The library.
Duh.

That's it, all right.
That's the same one that almost killed me back in the day.

You don't sound angry about it, sir.
Anger is a young person's game, Cardinal.
I'm just trying to make it to tomorrow.
WU-TANG

Well, we may have a lead on the invading ship's **occupants.**
On the bank of the reservoir, a sniffer team recovered a piece of wreckage that we think may have been used as a **raft.**
Think or know?
There's the rub, Grand Father.
We found multiple footprints in the sand, but our instruments are detecting absolutely no traces of human life.
They've learned to hide from us.
That's not good.
WU-TA
If enemy soldiers already escaped into our general population, shouldn't we alert the local authorities?
Hell, no.
If these kids have really figured out how to avoid detection, we need to ***question*** them.
And the Cleveland P.D. doesn't take prisoners.

Awesome.
We should blend right in with the roaming packs of feral young people.
Just act like you belong, new kid.

Does that mean *I'm* not "new kid" anymore?
Keep it down, new kid.
Our voices probably sound super old-timey to these people.
What are they all doing out in the middle of the night?
It *is* the middle of the night, isn't it?
Who can tell?
I guess Timbuk3 was right.
Heh.
Who the hell is Timbuk3?
Only the second cassette we ever bought with our own money.
One of the biggest bands in the world?
Jesus Christ, life is ephemeral.
Eryee eryee, btchz!

1ah tayka trip 2D passed?
Did she say...?
Don't engage.
Lady's probably just trying to sell us drugs.
1ah taysta whut d Cherch *updere* donshare?
God*all*, frum dino-meat 2 nic-heat.
Cigarettes.
Delicious, wholesome, cigare--
U!

HANDS!
BluLifes.
Don't...

RUN!
AAAHHH!
KZZOPP
BRAKOOOM

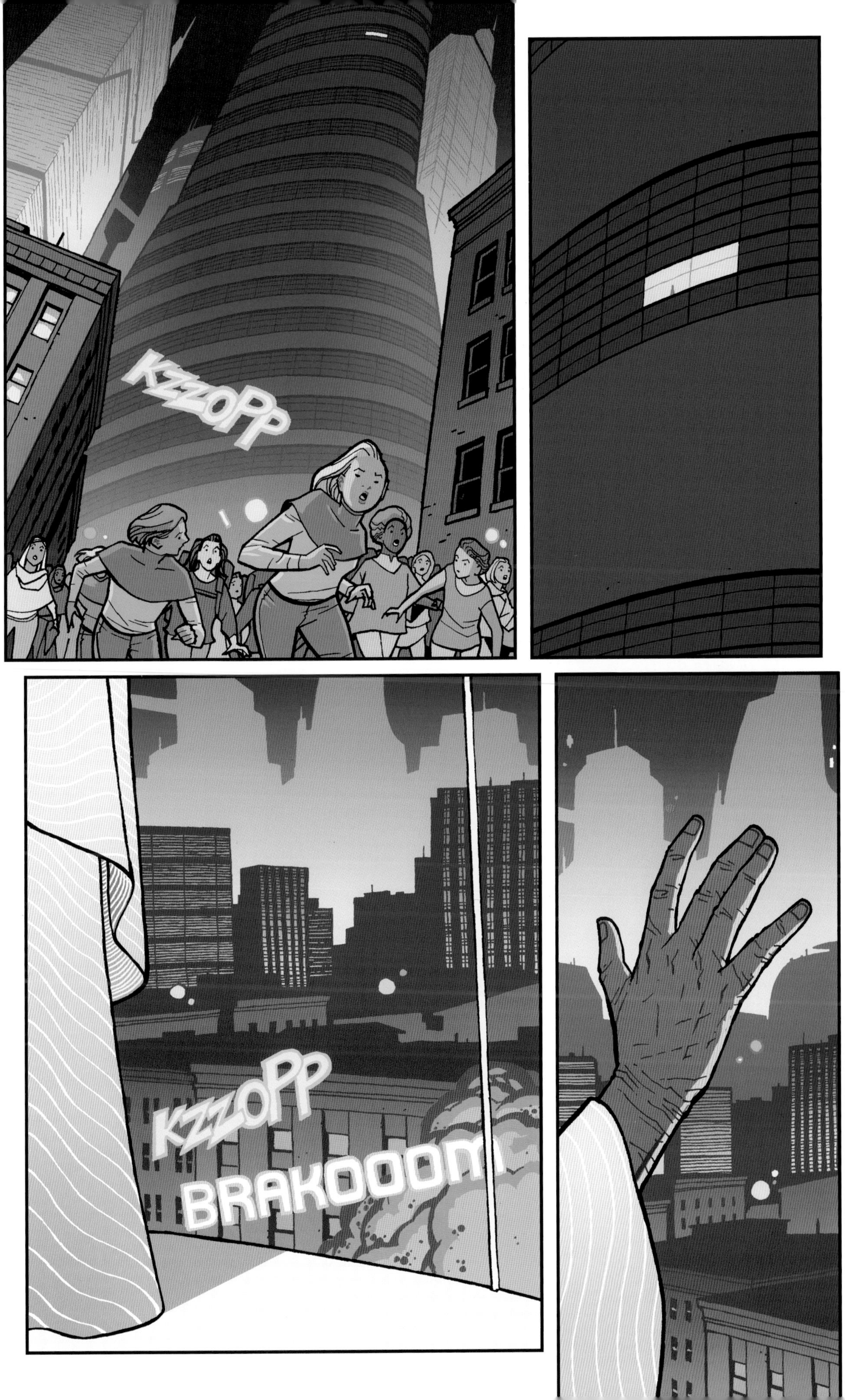
KZZOPP
KZZOPP
BRAKOOOM

THE CLEVELAND
THE CLEVELAND PUBLIC LIBRARY
Is everybody okay?
I...haven't run like that... since eighth grade...
How'd you know this joint was going to be *open* at this hour?
I didn't.
Figured we'd just smash a window or something.
That woman back there.
You think she *killed* those cops?
Unless they killed her first, I guess.
You guess? I'm seriously worried about what all this violence is doing to your brain, kid.
I mean, seeing *A Clockwork Orange* in high school really messes us up.

This place seems... popular.
What should we be looking for first?
Librarian.
Long time ago, I found out that they basically have to tell anyone who comes in anything that they...
...ask.

Hi.

Hello?
What *is* it?
Some kind of... animatronic plant.
I think it might be a ***computer.***
No.
It's the Tree of Knowledge.
And we should most ***definitely*** not touch it.
Why?
Um, have you ***read*** the Bible?
Nope.
Tree, what year is it?
It is the seventy-first year of the twenty-second century in the anno Domini designation.
Can I help you with anything else, MacKenzie?

How the heck does it know her name?
Don't waste your question on that!
It's not a genie with wishes, ding-dong. I think we get more than three.
Then we can ask it anything. We can ask it how to get **home.** We can ask about our own ***futures!***
Asking about ourselves is a really, really bad idea.
I kind of agree, actually.
Easy for you to say. You guys got to ***see*** how you turned out. And Mac already knows what happens to...
...sorry.
No, I like what you're getting at.
Tree, is there a cure for leukemia here in, what is it, 2171?
Indeed, that group of cancers has been eliminated.
Hell, yes.

CHAPTER 22

"This day and age we're living in
Gives cause for apprehension
With speed and new invention
And things like fourth dimension"

–From the 1931 song "As Time Goes By"
(verse unused in *Casablanca*)
Lyrics by Herman Hupfeld

Good evening, Wari.

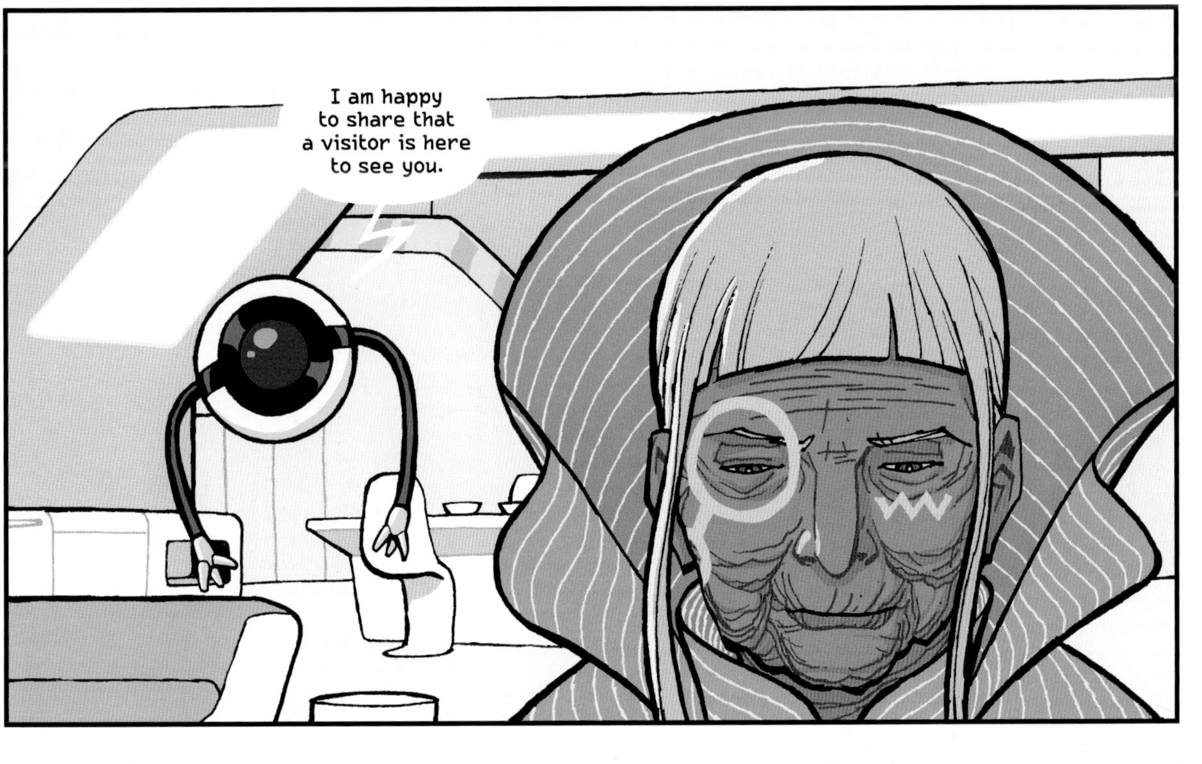
I am happy to share that a visitor is here to see you.

Tell him to go away, machine.
Of course, Wari. I will inform--
No, you won't.
Take a break, Caregiver.
My sister and I need to speak in private.
Certainly, Grand Father.
Good evening.
What do you want, Jahpo?
To find out what the hell is wrong with you.
The doctors told me you refused your treatment this morning.
I'm older than dirt, kid.
Now let me run out the clock in peace.

Can we please have this showdown literally any other night?
Work is a disaster at the moment.
What happened this time?
Sorry I brought it up.
Oh, you think I wouldn't understand your big, important job?
You're the one who's never had a clue about the truth, "baby brother."
And that's supposed to mean what, exactly?
Shentog tay!
Oochata madi tay!
Wari, you're speaking gibberish again.
If you keep skipping injections, it's only going to get--
BRRIIING

BRRIIIING
But, the only person who calls me on that contraption is *you.*
BRRIIING
Hello?
Sir, I know you said never to bother you when you're with family...
...but I thought this qualified as an emergency.
Just tell me what you have, Alister.
*It's the young **invaders** from another era.*
We found them.

I can't believe it.
I'm not gonna die.
Um, not to be a total wet blanket, Mac... but we don't ***know*** that for sure.

What the hell are you talking about, Erin?
That magic tree just said there's no leukemia in the future!
It wouldn't be the first time we've been *lied* to, KJ.
And even if what this thing said is true, what are we supposed to do?
Go to one of the dystopian drug stores out there and ask if they still have the *cure for cancer* in stock?
Isn't your mom a *doctor,* Tiffanies? All we have to do is find one, and they've taken some kind of *oath* to fix me, right?
I'm just saying, we shouldn't, you know...get our hopes up.
Heck and Naldo told us that our fate is our fate, that there's no changing when we die.
Oh, you mean the same two guys who used some future crap to save *your* life?
Yeah, fate can go fuck itself.
We're gonna make sure Mac lives to be a hundred.

And I'm all for that plan, really, but shouldn't we also figure out how to make it back to our own century?
Hey, Tree.
How do my friends and I get home to 1988?
Only those who have been ordained by WATCH are permitted to traverse space and/or time.
And how do we do whatever the heck it is you just said?
All four-dimensional itineraries must be approved by the organization's current leader, Jahpo Thāpā.
Jahpo...?
That was the name of Wari's baby!
Why do I never know what anyone is talking about?
Wari was our *friend*, a way-too-young mom we met back in, like, dinosaur times.
And "Jahpo" isn't exactly a name you see on the back of a lot of bicycles. If this isn't a coincidence...
Cards.

Cards, please.

Jesus!
What *is* it?
A freaking monster!
Actually, I think it might be some kinda ***robot.***
Uh-uh.
It's the librarian.
Valid cards are required to visit the branches.
Tiffany.
Do you still have your--
Shhh.
I'm on it.

fzzt
That antique does not belong to you.
That antique must be cataloged.
No problem.
Thing was killing my back anyway.
You can *have* it.

Holy cow.
That was--
kssh
kssh
kssh
Oh.

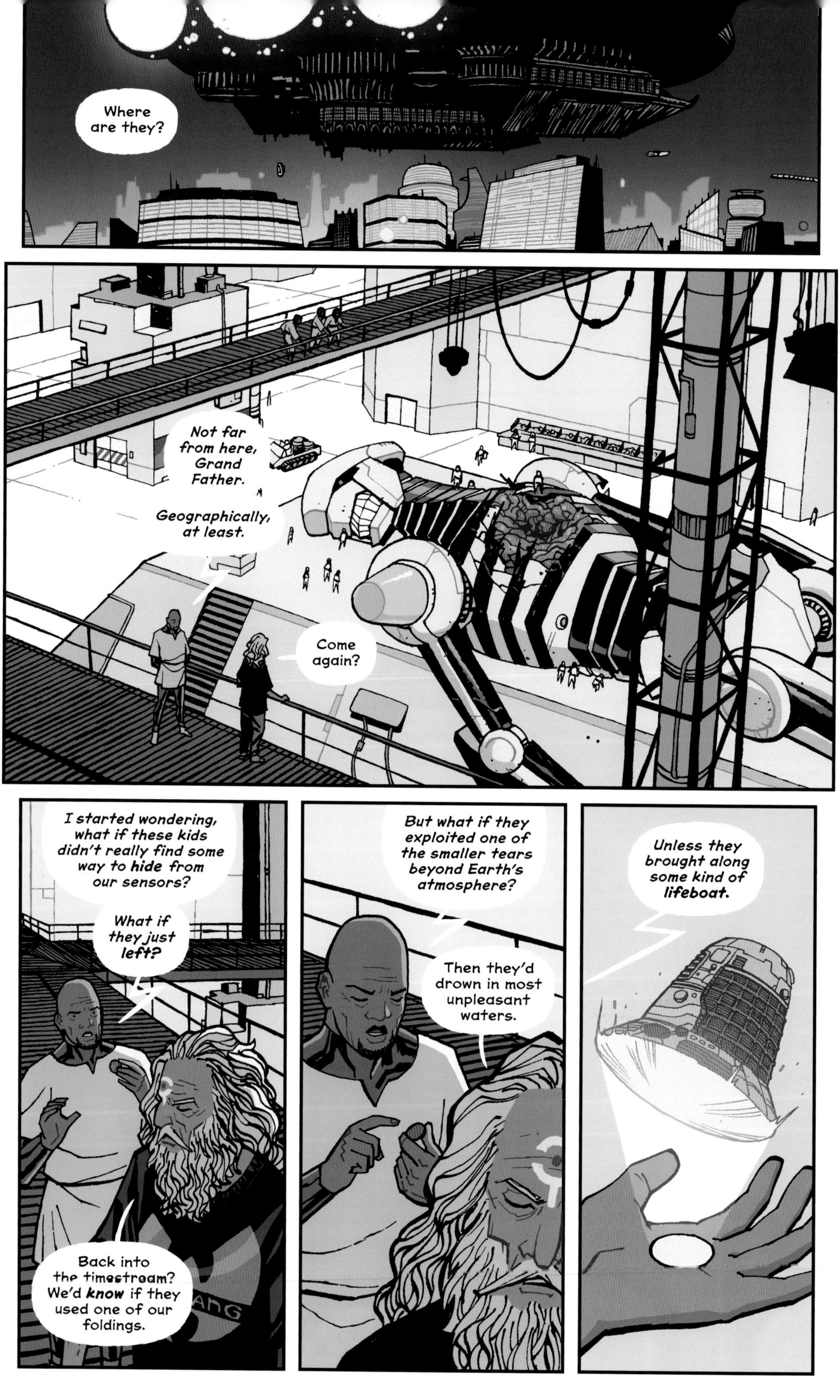
Where are they?
Not far from here, Grand Father.
Geographically, at least.
Come again?
I started wondering, what if these kids didn't really find some way to hide from our sensors?
What if they just left?
Back into the timestream? We'd know if they used one of our foldings.
But what if they exploited one of the smaller tears beyond Earth's atmosphere?
Then they'd drown in most unpleasant waters.
Unless they brought along some kind of lifeboat.

How...?
I had the Altar Girls scrub every second of stealth-sat footage from yesterday back to the Industrial Revolution.
They finally spotted this object entering the atmosphere above a residential district formerly known as Stony Stream sometime in the fall of 1988.
WU-TANG
And you're sure these are the same monsters who killed Prioress?
Not without physical evidence, which is why I'd like to make a **scouting report.**
If these **are** your troublemakers, we may need to send considerable backup to perform Ablution on the entire zone.
I'll be damned.
I expected the brats to run...
...but I never thought they'd get so far.

Cleveland
So what do we do now that Tiff broke the entire library?
Hey, I saved us from killer Claymation!
You also threw away the only weapon we had to defend ourselves.
If there's any chance that Wari and Jahpo are really here, I vote we try to find them.
They'd be like a million years old by now!
Then I guess we should start looking in nursing homes.
I'll second starting with a familiar face.
If Wari found some way to bring her kid here, she probably also knows how we can leave.
You guys can do whatever you want, but *I'm* gonna help Mac find her super-medicine.
It's all right, Kaje. We can take care of my stuff later. Best to stick together.
Actually, *splitting up* is probably a better idea.

Are you nuts?
Splitting up is always the stupidest idea!
Unless anyone out there is looking for a group of five chicks from another era, in which case it's definitely the smartest play.
And we could always use your *walkies* to stay in touch.
You've been lugging those things around this whole time?!
What, Tiffany said they were *expensive.*
This packrat hasn't even dumped her old papers yet!
Don't listen to these ingrates, Tieng.
You saved my *babies.*
kzzzt
Sounds like no one's using these frequencies anymore, so the airwaves are all ours.
But I don't know who might be listening in, so let's not use our real names or anything, okay?

10-4, good buddy.
But what if we run out of batteries or whatever?
As long as we only use them for emergencies, these radios should both be good for at least a few more hours.
But just in case anything goes sideways, we should all plan to meet back here.
At let's say... dawn?
Good luck, assholes.
Good luck, assholes.
Stay safe, dummies.
Stay safe, dummies.
Over and out.

Cleveland Clinic
Downtown

You sure whatever we've been following is an ambulance?
What else would it be, Kaje?
Some kind of futuristic *hearse,* maybe?
Why would they be bringing a dead body *back* to a hospital?
How do we even know this place *is* a hospital?
With our luck, it's gonna turn out to a be a *snake store.*
Gotta start somewhere.
Mac, wait.
Before we do this... there's something I have to tell you.

That's never good.
It's about that thing from another dimension.
The...the one that touched me.
And made you hallucinate about the future?
It *wasn't* a hallucination, Mac.
Isn't that what all crazy people say?
Listen to me, goddammit!
I saw Doctor Braunstein's face covered in blood, and that *happened*.
I saw a skyline that looked exactly like this one, and now we're *here*.
And I also saw something about *us*.

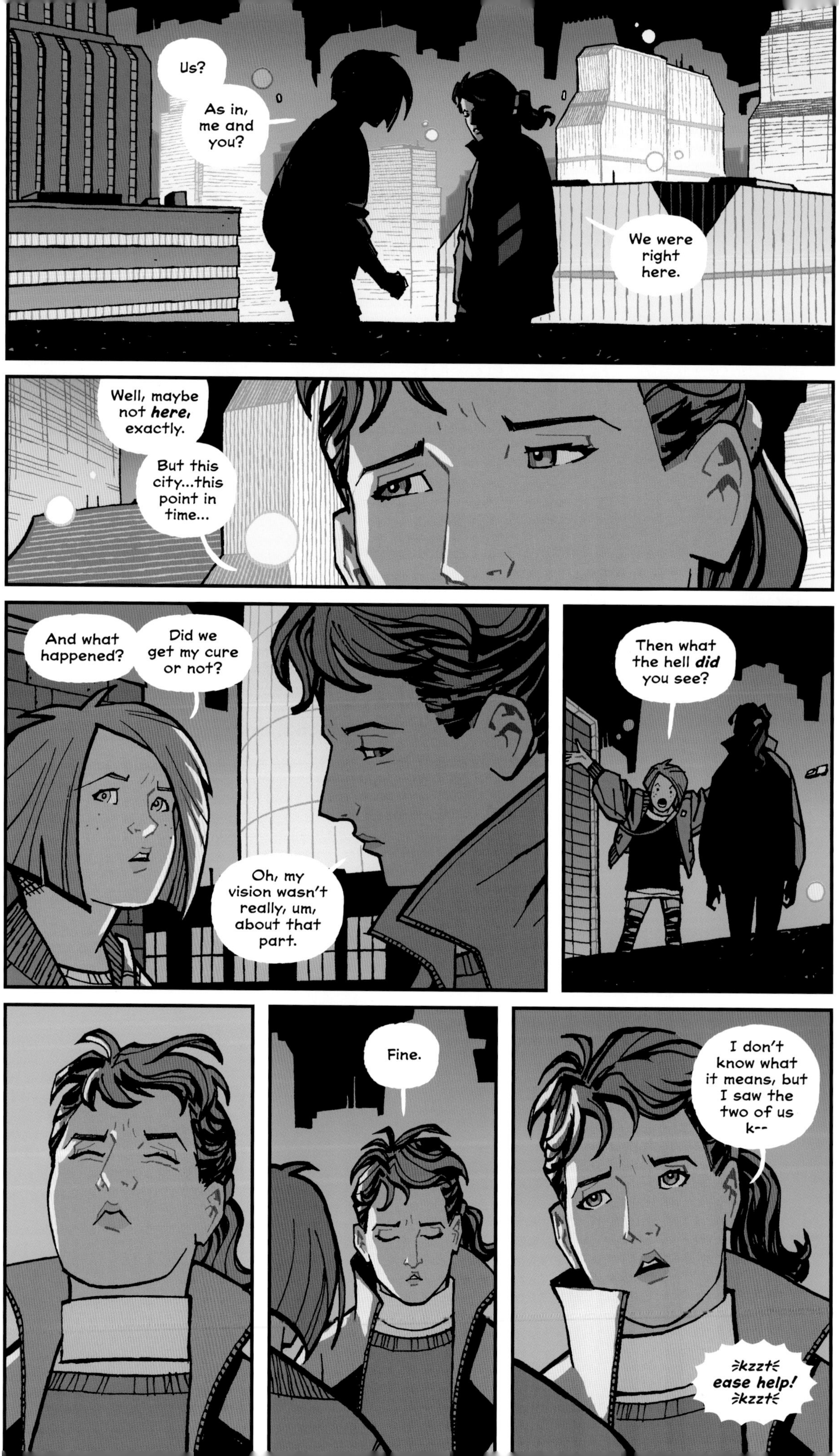
Us?
As in, me and you?
We were right here.
Well, maybe not *here*, exactly.
But this city...this point in time...
And what happened?
Did we get my cure or not?
Oh, my vision wasn't really, um, about that part.
Then what the hell *did* you see?
Fine.
I don't know what it means, but I saw the two of us k--
kzzt
ease help!
kzzt

Those guys are *already* in trouble?
kzzt e to the kzzt
Say again?
We can barely hear y--
EEEEEEE
What *is* that?
EEEEEEEEE
I don't know, but I think I've heard it before.
At Erin's house, back when all this--
kzzt Please help! Oh, Christ, she's dead! She's really kzzt
Who... who was that?
How do you not recognize that voice?

It was *you.*

CHAPTER 23

6’0”

5’6”

5’0”

4’6”

4’0”

3’6”

3’0”

"Yet we get a trifle weary
With Mr. Einstein's theory
So we must get down to earth at times
Relax, relieve the tension"

–From the 1931 song "As Time Goes By"
(verse unused in *Casablanca*)
Lyrics by Herman Hupfeld

Careful.

I wouldn't go in there if I was you.
Yeah, well, I'm kind of the only person in this trio who *isn't* you, Tiffany.
Besides, I've had a lot of luck finding people with phonebooks.
That was in the past, Erin!
And we don't even know if this thing *is* a phone booth!
Maybe it's another time machine? Like in *Bill & Ted's*?
Who the heck are Bill and Ted?
Seriously?
Thought I'd already seen that by '88...
FSSSSS
Uh-oh.

Shit!
We've got to break her out of there!
Non!
U crays 1ah bringbak de BluLifes?!
Is that the same huckster lady from before?
We were sure those cops killed you!
Um, help, please?!
Ducalm.
Yusta KleenBox.
4d huggerz?

Not more giant insects...
More?!
koff
I think she means that thing was for **delousing...** like when my entire third grade got head lice?
U3 talklike Cherch kin.
Wear u btchz frum?
Uh...
My sisters and I are from **Canada.**
Cuckos?
How'd you get over the wall?
You can understand us?
Please, my friends and I are trying to find a woman named **Wari.**

Only person I've ever heard with that handle is Wari Thāpā.
Sister of that WATCH asshole Jahpo.
Sister?
The Wari we met was Jahpo's mother.
Whatever, do you know where we could find her?
No clue.
But The Preserver did a puff piece on her a few months back.
Newspapers are still a thing?
Hey, I recognize that building behind her.
It's not far from--
WHOOP
WHOOP

Pigs are making another pass.
Scatter!
Wait!
It's okay.
We got what we needed.
We did?
kzzzt
kzzt Michelangelo to Donatello, can you hear me Donatello? kzzt
Loud and clear, Mikey.
You and Raphael have any luck yet?

I still don't get why New Kid is Leonardo.
I mean, Leo is the *leader.*
We're still on the move, but listen, did you guys just hear anything... ***weird*** on your walkie?
Uh, negative, this is the first peep we've heard out of our radio since we split up, why?
Rad.
We'll call you back when we have anything to report, over and out.
You didn't want to maybe give them a heads-up that we just heard ***you*** say somebody was ***dead?!***
That's what ***you*** heard, KJ.
It could have been any chick's voice, or just your imagination.
Mac...
Those ambulance guys left an entrance open.
Should be easier than talking our way past some psycho nurse at the front desk, so let's roll.

I'm just saying, if that really was some kind of...of future broadcast, the person you were saying was dead is probably *me.*
Kaje, the kid most likely to croak next is still ***yours truly.***
So let's grab this anti-leukemia juice and get the hell out of here.
You sure you don't want to wait until we hear anything else?
Why?
Aren't you the one who had some sort of premonition about this wacky time zone?
Yeah.
And?
Were either of us dead in your vision?
Uh-uh.
We were... romantic.

The two of us?
As in, you and me...?
Yeah.
That's *disgusting.*
I'm so sorry.
I didn't mean to--
Don't touch me!

If you want to grow up to be a pervert, I can't stop you.
But it's got jack to do with *me*, get it?
Got it.
Good.
Come on.
Coming.

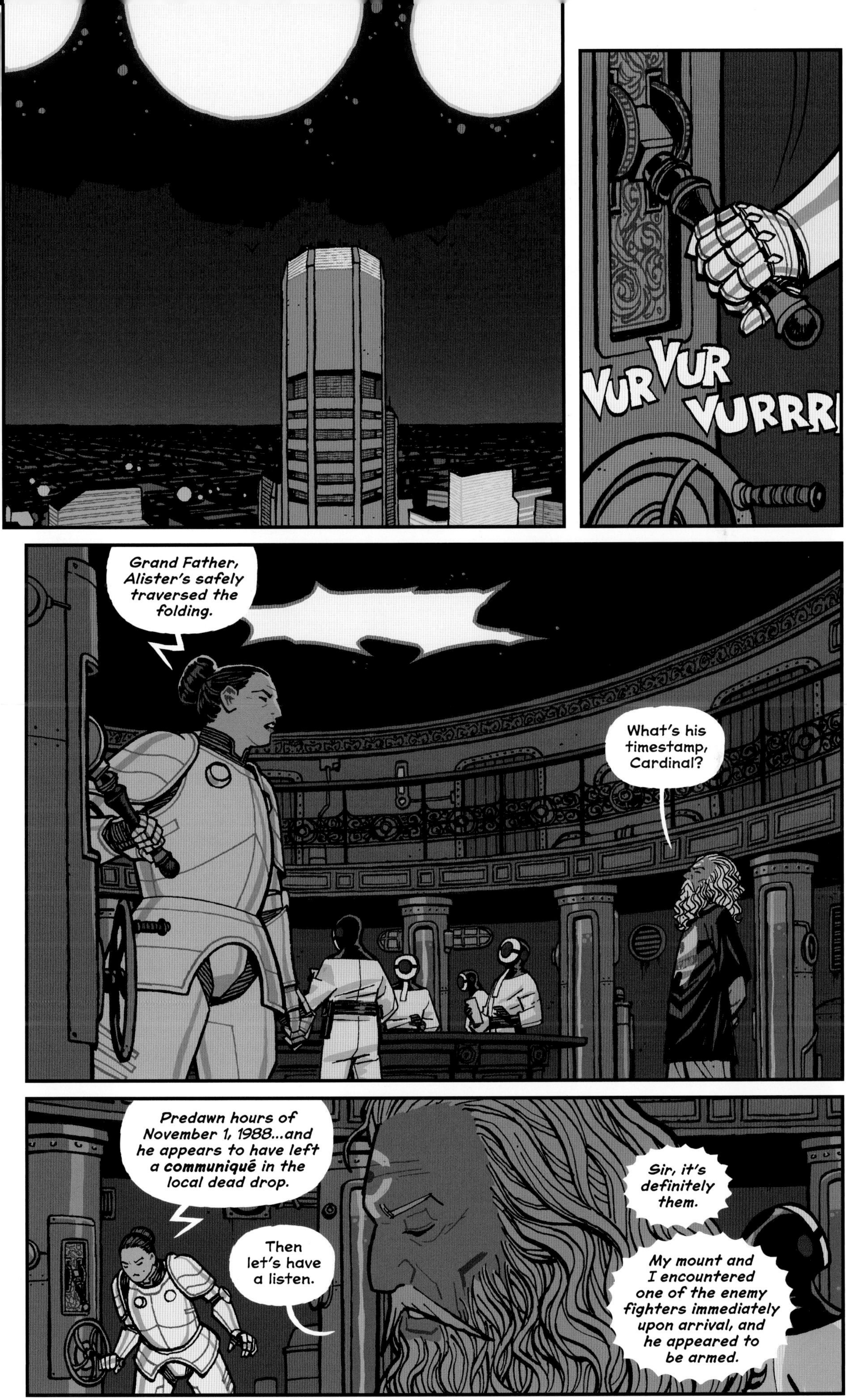
VUR VUR VURRR
Grand Father, Alister's safely traversed the folding.
What's his timestamp, Cardinal?
Predawn hours of November 1, 1988...and he appears to have left a **communiqué** in the local dead drop.
Then let's have a listen.
Sir, it's definitely them.
My mount and I encountered one of the enemy fighters immediately upon arrival, and he appeared to be armed.

I'm afraid we had no choice but to engage.

True to form, it looks as if the little thief and his accomplices have been pilfering archaic **hardware** from each era they've invaded...
...including this one.
I'll begin the hunt for the others, but this sector has clearly been **tainted**, so my personal recommendation would be for WATCH to dispatch considerable...
...reinforcements?
Dear old Grand Father.
Always one step ahead.

ding
Let's just try one more floor.
Fine, but five bucks says it's going to be exactly as empty as all the others.
Trust me, this is definitely the right place.
Says who? No doormen means this probably isn't an apartment building, and no janitors means it's not an office complex.
Face it, this skyscraper is nothing but *haunted.*
Please don't tell me I grow up to believe in ghosts.
What, like undead spirits would be any less insane than everything else we've--
Good evening.
AHHH!

How are you, Erin Tieng?
How... how do you know my--
Apologies.
This is a private residence.
Strangers are not permitted.

Hgh!
Kkt!
LET THEM GO!
No thank you.
Do... something...

Don't... help... me!
Help... her!
If she dies... I don't... exist!
That's right.
If you're still alive, that means your younger self can't--
Stop it, goddammit.

Turn yourself off, machine.
Of course, Wari.
Hhhhhh!
It's... it's really her.
koff koff koff
Wari, it's me, **Erin.**
I don't know if you remember, but we met, like, thousands of years ago. I was the girl from the future? Well, it **used** to be the future, but now I guess it's your--
How could I forget you, silly **oorashi?**
You were just here the other day.
Oh.
Wait.
Huh?

Cleveland Clinic
Downtown
STAFF ONLY
NO PATIENTS
What the fuck's up, doc?

Dahell B U?
You don't need to know who we are.
You speak Olde English?
And you do, too, huh?
Awesome, 'cause I'm just looking for some kinda **booster shot,** and then I promise we'll be out of your hair.
sigh
Open your mouth.
ahhhhhh
That's what I thought.
There's nothing I can do for you.

Why not?!
Because this young woman has no ***inSure* chip.**
I can't treat anyone without proper coverage.
Bullshit.
Kaje, what are you doing?!
Saving your life.
SECURI--
Don't.
You wouldn't be the first guy I've killed, understand?
I...I understand.
Cool.
You help my friend stay alive, I do the same for you.

Badass.

CHAPTER 24

"No matter what the progress
Or what may yet be proved
The simple facts of life are such
They cannot be removed"

-From the 1931 song "As Time Goes By"
(verse unused in *Casablanca*)
Lyrics by Herman Hupfeld

I'm going home!

Mmn?
Wari, get up!
You have to see this!
H'achati?
I don't know, maybe those four girls actually managed to get word to my company.
Or maybe some archeologist in 2055 just dug up **this thing.**
--name is Doctor Qanta Braunstein, and I am stranded in the year 11,705 BCE, having lost my only--
Either way, the future finally threw me a lifeline.

So.
You now leave me?
Assuming that Beta Model is operational... yeah.
But I will never forget everything you've done for me these past--
Bullshit!
Cha vera cee rata, zu heeli!
Slow down, honey.
I can't understand what you're--
Jahpo.
My baby.
You taking him *with.*

Wari.
I...I wish I could, but my time would never allow that.
Then go other time.
Other place.
My people, they have *rules,* rules I've already broken...
Please!
Jahpo not survive his *fathers* one more winters.
I don't know.
I...I don't know how.
I can show.

And I did.
Holy crap.
"Mother" took my son *and* me with her to Indonesia, years after her colleagues here in the States had stopped looking for her.
Her only condition was that I never tell anyone when or where we *really* came from...including Jahpo, who she raised as her own.
Which is probably why the *orchadee* kid turned out to be such a little *dekfek*.
This is amazing, Wari, really.
But, what did you mean when you said that you'd just seen me the *other day?*
...
Who the hell are you girls, and how did you get in my house?
Ummmmm
Ma'am, my friends and I are just like you, products of another era.
You were about to tell us if you still had this...this *Time Capsule* you used to escape the past?

Ah.
Now I remember.
Your name is Erin Tieng.
You came here a few months ago to *give* me something.
I did? How? ***What?***
Where did I put whatever it was, machine?
I'm sorry, Wari.
I am unable to say.
We are never getting home.
Oh my God, is this real?!
The President of the United States is ***black?!***

Sure, lots of 'em have been.
Are you serious?!
Since when?!
Spoiler alert!
I mean, maybe it's gonna happen in our life-times!
Is that even possible?!
And what is a "spoiler alert"?!
I know it's around here somewhere...
kzzt Leonardo, come in. kzzt
You gotten us a ride home yet or what?
Uh, not exactly, Raphael.
How are you guys doing...?

I think we're close to a breakthrough, so step on it.
Over and out.
The...the instruments are primed, miss.
Ready when you girls are.
You doing okay, Mac?
This is creepier than my gym teacher testing us for scoliosis.
But if it's gonna zap out my disease, then let her rip.

You sure this is safe, Doc?
Completely.
After I finish this scan, the Gene-E will eliminate any...
Hmm.
"Hmm?"
What the hell does "hmm" mean?!
This shouldn't be possible...
Is it good news or what?
This young woman doesn't have leukemia.
She never did, and she never will.
That's... that's amazing news.
Right?

I don't know who gave her that diagnosis, but they had no idea how to read a nucleolus.
The untreatable disease your friend is eventually going to develop is actually called *4DC*.
Untreatable?
It's a rare group of cancers that only afflicts a small percentage of certain professionals...
...*time travelers*.
RESTRAINT
HEY!
kashunk
kashunk

Let her go!
I thought you backwater btchz were just immigrants.
But you're *invaders*, aren't you?
Step away from there or you're a dead man!
I already am.
Do you have any idea what WATCH does to people who *help* you whores?
Killing you is my only shot at living.
fsssss
KJ!

tink
It's just a sedative, don't fight it.
I promise to wait until you're both unconscious before the next step.
koff koff
You won't feel a thing.
Kaje!
Your boots!

VMMMMMM
VMMMMMMM

nnnn...
Creep.
You are seriously my hero.
I seriously... need a nap...
Don't pass out on me yet.
We gotta jet before Dr. No-Nards comes to.
But your treatment--
--was always a pipedream.
The new kid was right, you die when you die.
But that ain't gonna be today.

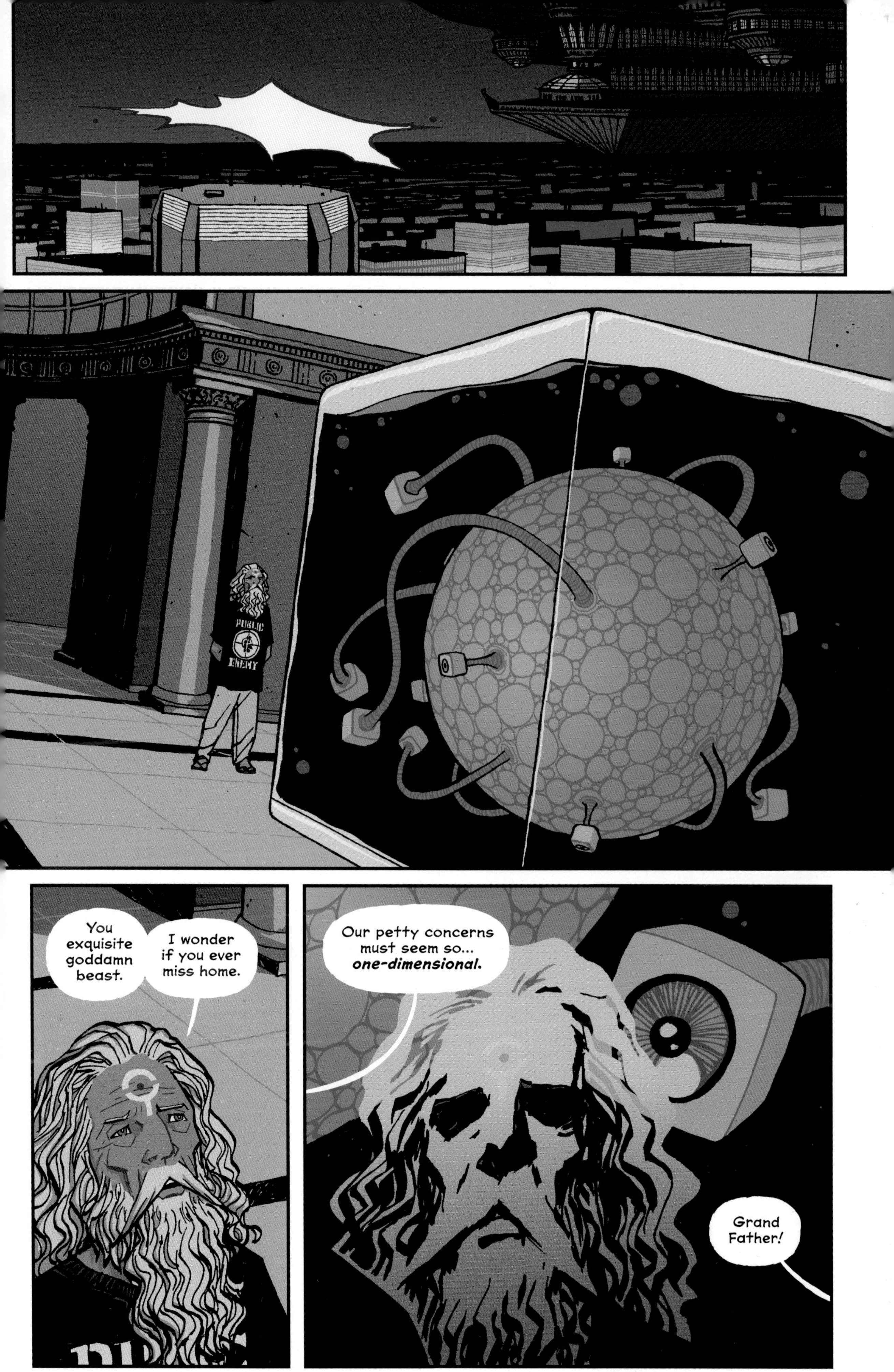
PUBLIC ENEMY
You exquisite goddamn beast.
I wonder if you ever miss home.
Our petty concerns must seem so... **one-dimensional.**
Grand Father!

Maxima for d ruption, but...
oh
She won't bite.
Just tell us what's happening, minus the slanguage, if you please.
PUBLIC
Switchboard got a call from a local physician who says he encountered two juvenile enemy fighters.
At a hospital? Cardinal, how many calls a day do we get about mentally ill patients who think they're lost in time?
PUBLIC
And I know we'd normally kick this to the cops, but with those teenagers still on the loose--
Your best scout is confident they're all in 1988.
And I'm beginning to think we should join him there.
Tell helm to take us into the folding.
Wait a minute.
You're bringing the whole Cathedral into the past?

An entire community has been *exposed.*
We need to start processing them in bulk.
What about just taking a few of the bots?
They leave too much of a footprint.
If we have to violate another year, we should do it as cleanly as current technology allows.
But you're potentially exposing every last member of WATCH to--
Do you think these things picked me to *listen?!*
Sorry.
Long day.
Why... why don't you get some rest, sir?
I'll wake you when it's time.

Forgive my memory, old friends.
If you say it's here, we'll find it, Wari.
Unless this lady is speaking nonsense, which she most definitely is.
Wait a second.
This man.
This is Jahpo?
Nowadays, he goes by "Grand Father."
A title my foolish son believes he *earned*.
I've seen him before. Back when this all started.
He was the old-timer outside that house the first time we all--
Help!

Please.
This chick is ≥hnn≤ surprisingly heavy.
Are you two all right?
Nuh muh nuh.
I'm fine, but K...but whatever-her-codename-is is sorta out of it.
Long story, but I got her as far as some roof on Euclid.
Think we're where the old *Arcade* used to be.
I could use a hand getting her wherever you guys are.
Copy that, Mikey.
Just keep her safe until we get there.
Ten-fucking-four.

Team Tiffany can handle this.
We can?
You stay here and keep looking. Let us know what you find.
Are... are you sure?
If anyone can figure out what the heck is going on, it's you.
Be careful out there, young ladies.
This city isn't as safe as it used to be.
Ha!

Would you care for some more *pisang goreng?*
Um, no thanks.
Hey, are you positive you don't know where Wari hid whatever it is we're supposed to be looking for?
I'm sorry.
I am unable to say.
What's my favorite color?
I regret that I do not know the answer to that question.
Wari, did you hear?
Your pet robot doesn't know my favorite color!
So what?
So, if you ask it about what I left you, it doesn't say that, it says it's "unable to say."
I think it knows ***something,*** but it's, like, not allowed to tell us!

Any chance it works like an ATM?
Maybe you need to enter some kind of *code?*
Not a code... a password.
Dreamwomen.
Here is the document you asked me to protect, Erin Tieng.
The what?
It's a... *a map.*
A map to where?
Home.

CHAPTER 25

"You must remember this
A kiss is still a kiss
A sigh is just a sigh
The fundamental things apply
As time goes by"

–From the 1931 song "As Time Goes By"
Lyrics by Herman Hupfeld

Are they there yet?
That's a big fat negative.
Sleepy and I are still waiting for the Tiffanies, or whatever I'm supposed to be calling th--
Okay, cool, that's fine, actually. As soon as they get there, tell them to **forget** coming back here.
Can you see the skyscraper with the glow-y thing above it?
Kinda hard to miss.
Cool, well, there's something called a "service entrance" in the alley right behind that building, and you guys all need to meet me there, like, immediately.
It's our last chance of getting back to ≶KzzZZzzzt≶
Erin...?

So that's the plan?
FAHH!
Almost pissed myself, jerk.
I thought you were still high on that goofball spray.
Must have worn off. I feel like a million...
...oh.
What's up, Kaje?
This place.
It's... it's...
...it's *nothing.*
All of this has been completely pointless.
No matter what we do, you're still gonna *die.*

Are you seriously crying?
Knock it off, dweeb.
It's bullshit, Mac!
Why did we get sucked into this stupid adventure?
Just so you could get some kind of goddamn ***time travel cancer?***
Look, if somebody had to catch it, I'm just glad it was me and not one of you guys.
Mostly you.
So that's it?
Our stories are already written, and... and there's nothing we can do to change them?
I suppose.
Like, this rooftop.
This is where you had your vision of us ***kissing...*** isn't it?

Then I guess we do.

Sorry to...
Um.
Congratulations?
U4!
HANDS!

I did this.
Be here at 7:17 AM!
This is totally my handwriting.
Of course it is.
You asked us to protect it the first time you came to visit, Erin Tieng.
How do I learn all this stuff about access codes and secret elevators?
Well, my memory's not what it used to be, but maybe I lend a hand.
This looks just like my boy's old clubhouse.
Haven't been there since Jahpo abandoned it for his new toy, but I still remember a few things.
This map supposedly shows me how to get back to 1988.
If it really works, how do I end up back here in the future--I mean, your past--to give it to you?
...
Who are you again?

Forget it.
My note says I have to get the others to the top of that tower before 7:17 this morning.
That's when the main window WATCH uses always closes for realignment.
Maybe it's open to your time now.
Then this thing must actually be right...like when I carved that message on KJ's stick to warn Past Us!
Come again?
If this works, sounds like I will.
See you later, Wari!
Watch your back, child!
It's not just my son's soldiers you have to worry about out there!
Don't forget, these boys are at war!

Hell.
U!
DROP WEAPON!
What?! This isn't a--
KABANG
Last warn.
ROP WEAPON
You fired a fucking gun?
At children?

ON KNEES!
KNEEL
Just do what he says!
Yeah, I remember thinking like that.
Take care of your friends.
And whatever you do, don't settle.
Wait, what is she--
RAAHHH!

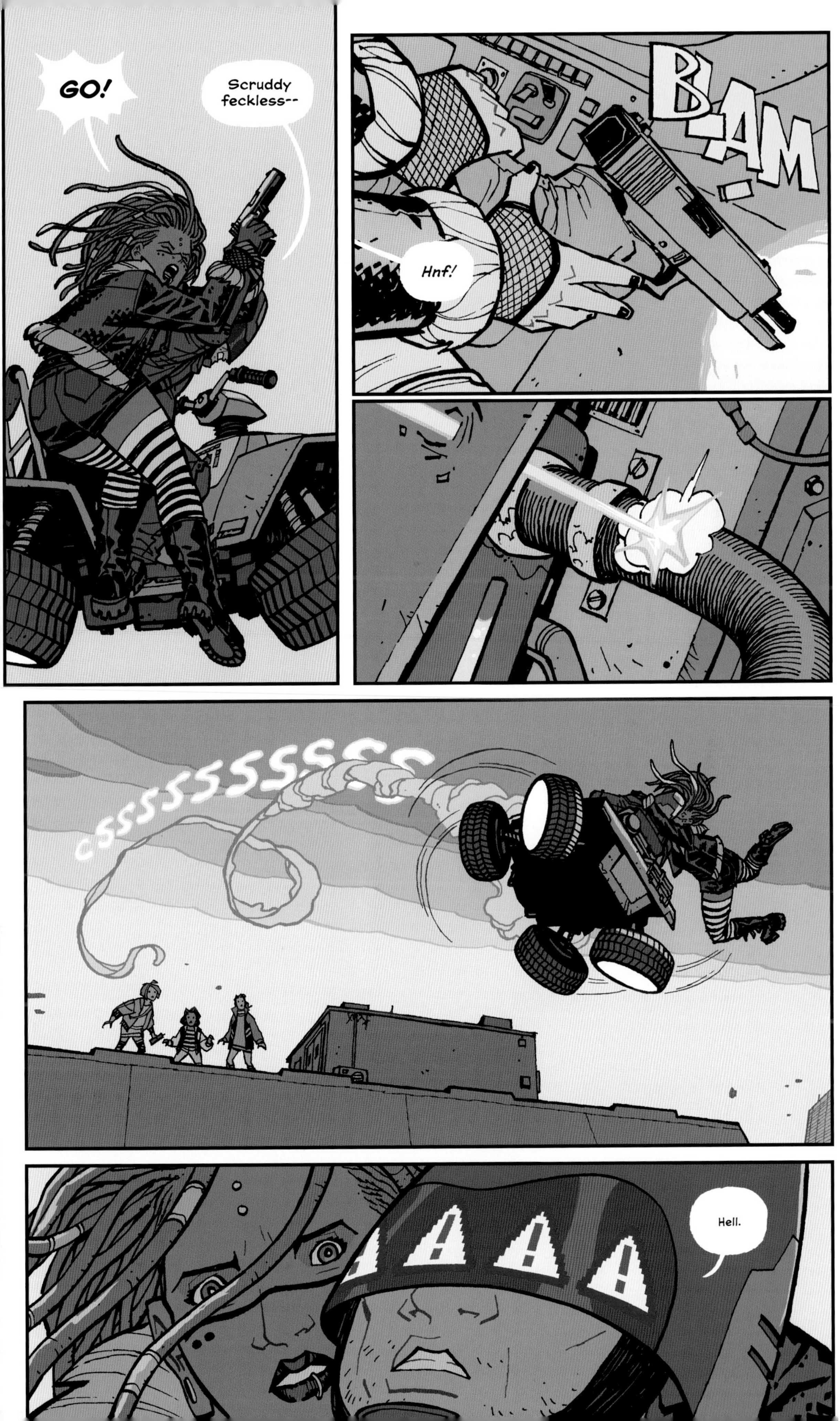
GO!
Scruddy feckless--
BLAM
Hnf!
CSSSSSSSSSSS
Hell.

NO!
Erin! Anybody!
Please, help!
Oh Christ, she's dead!
She's really--
EEEEEEE
Dammit!
Tiffany, I am...I am so, *so* sorry.
Me too, but we gotta move.
That bang's only gonna bring more of those assholes, and if we get nabbed now...
...what did Tiff die for?

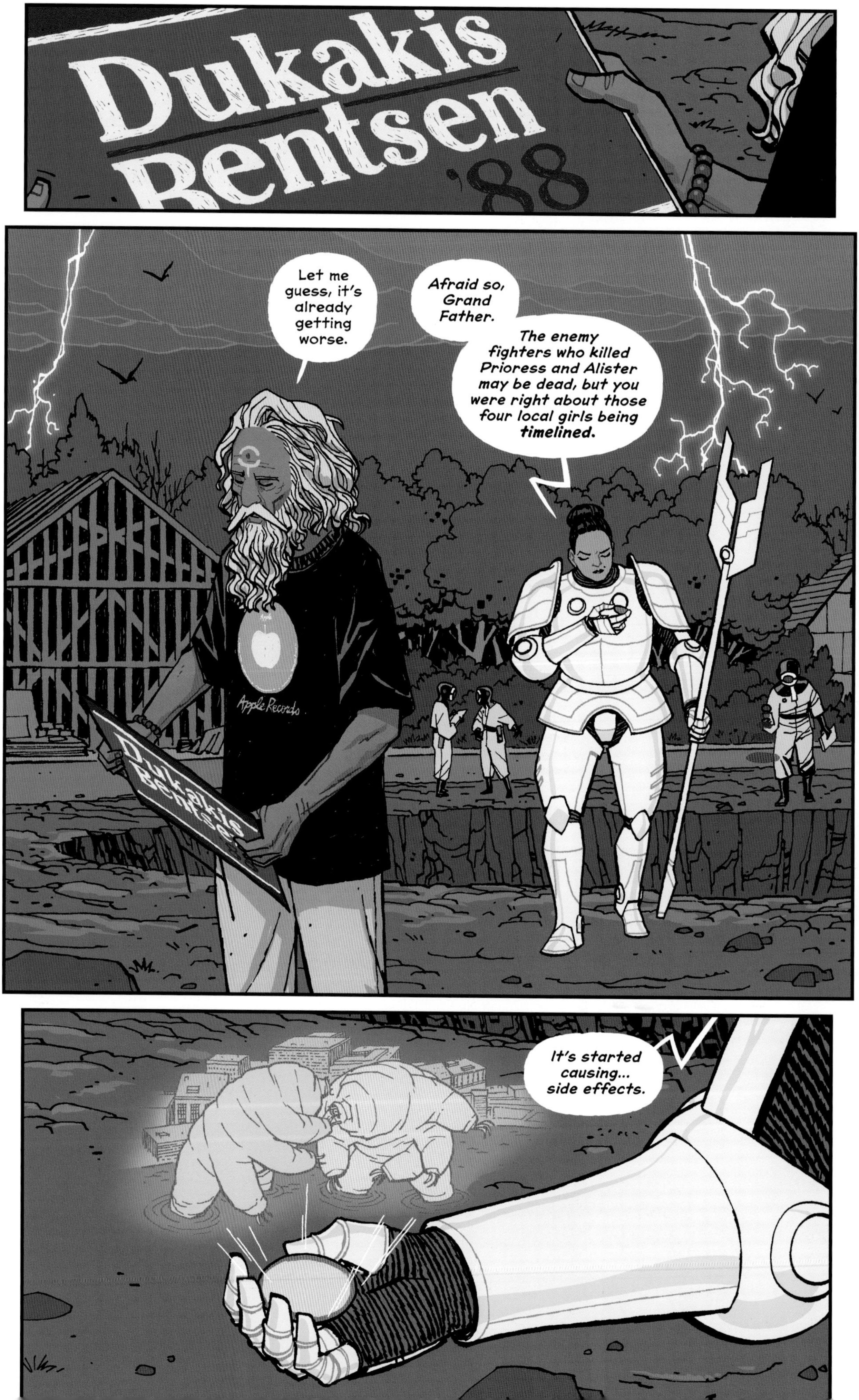

Dukakis
Bentsen
'88
Let me guess, it's already getting worse.
Afraid so, Grand Father.
The enemy fighters who killed Prioress and Alister may be dead, but you were right about those four local girls being **timelined.**
Apple Records
It's started causing... side effects.

Kālī beyond.
When is this?
Altar Girls are still triangulating, but it's roughly twenty-eight years ahead of our current position.
Then it's spreading even faster than I feared.
Call everyone back to the Cathedral.
So now we're breaking curfew? I thought--
Cardinal, if we don't find those four children and bring them back here alive, this entire year is going to bend *inside* itself.
Wouldn't that mean the end of *time?*
Oh, no matter what we do, time will keep on ticking.
This will just be the end of the world.
Apple Records

Yes!
Man, I'm so glad to see you.
Hurry, we have to be on the top of this thing at the exact right corner before...
Where's Double-oh Tiff?
No more stupid nicknames, New Kid.
We lost her.
Lost...?
I think I just watched myself die.
But.
No.

It's true, Erin.
Uh-uh.
Whatever happened, we...we can *fix* it.
Trust us, we can't.
I hate to say it, but you were right about me. About ***death.*** When we go is when we go.
Unless it's not!
Listen, I know it's confusing, but at some point, I'm gonna show up here a few weeks back to draw this map for Wari. So she can eventually give it to me, right?
But now, I'll add a ***note*** to my past self...one warning the Tiffanies about what just happened!
Could that work?
You're asking ***me?***
It doesn't add up.
If you're the one who's eventually going to draw that thing, why doesn't it say all this stuff already?
ding

Holy cow.

I can't believe that worked.

Oh, God.
It's you!
Evil clone you.
Just so you know, in the future, that kind of talk is gonna sound ultra-bigoted.
But nice to see the crew again. Been stalking you for ages, literally.
Thankfully, you left behind plenty of clues on this pitstop, so once I figured out what you were up to, I dropped in first to start laying some groundwork.
The map. You drew it for Wari.
Thought it would take forever to learn your lousy penmanship, but turns out that's a nature over nurture kinda thing.
Why?
Why do all this to get us here?
Because I'm just a kid.
And I'm tired of fighting.
00:32

Is that...?
I need this to end, all right?
But if I let you four go back to '88 together, the old-timers will have won.
ARMED
Look, we'll do whatever you want, join your nightmare future army, anything.
Please, don't... don't blow us up.
Not today.
Sorry.
You girls are just no good together.
klik

...what?

The Cleveland Preserver
IRAQ BECOMES REPUBLIC AFTER MILITARY COUP
Fate of King Unknown as Pro-Egyptian Junta Rules
Hi.
The Cleveland Preserver

LLRRXXXX

Hey, lady.
You okay?

CHAPTER

26

BOO
RIP

APPLE PIE
APPLE PIE
THE BODY OF CHRIST!
Wait.
You want me to eat this?
Does it get me kicked out of paradise... or invited in?
Damn, remember when those things used to be fried?
APPLE PIE

In the future, they're gonna be baked.
And they *suck.*
Missy.
How do you know about the *future?*
Sorry, Mom says I'm not supposed to talk about stuff that makes you anxious.
So I'll just put you out of your mis
APPLE PIE

My hero.
Don't get too attached, new kid.
Turns out I'm not the man you think I am.
Now listen up, I came all this way to tell you something important.
If you want to get back home, you have to ***moonwalk,*** understand?
This is a dream.
This is a dream and I totally know that I'm dreaming.
No, this is a ***message,*** and if you forget...
...we're all gonna burn in ***hell.***

hhht
AHHH!
It's okay, Erin.
You're safe now.
What is this?
How do you know my *name?!*

My son said you *fainted.*
And we found your "A.N.D.G." card.
Whoa.
I didn't even know they still *made* those.
THE AMERICAN NEWSPAPER DELIVERY GUILD
SINCE 1899!
MEMBERSHIP CARD
Erin Tieng
YOUR NAME
3905137
MEMBER ID
Where's your squad?
My what?
Your friends. You trick-or-treating *alone?*
No. I...I don't know. There was some kind of *explosion* and--
Dad!
The sky is all wrong!
...moonwalk...

POP
Umm, what just happened?

Sorry, Grand Father.
We left 002016 at our usual trajectory, but we seem to have been waylaid.
In what bloody year?
That's the thing, sir.
We're not in a specific time, we're... interstitial.
We're *inside* the fourth dimension?
Well, "inside" is a relative term, but--
How the devil do we get out?
According to the last transmission we were able to receive from back home, our Main Folding seems to have been **closed**.
By what?
By whom, actually.

Five youths, but that's all I can tell you.
Instruments weren't even able to detect their basic vitals, much less make any positive identifications, though a few of them seem...familiar.
Cardinal, what if this is them?
The four girls we lost in '88.
What if we all just passed each other?
Some of their garb matches the era.
But what about this one? She's dressed more like one of our shitty descendants.
And if an enemy fighter found these poor kids before us...
Did...did that animal just murder innocent civilians?
Worse, she weaponized them.
I don't follow.
By scattering these girls to different corners of the hypercube, she didn't just bend a single year inside itself, she--
RUVRUV
RUUVV

That's... not one of ours.
Breach!
Huh.
Grand Father, all hands are struggling just to batten down the Cathedral.
We're in no shape to repel invaders!
Yeah, well, the future is never fair.
Just inevitable.

Awesome.
Where the hell am I this time?
Did you fellas hear that?
The girl, she...she *cussed.*
1958?
Guess it could have been worse.
Right over there.
I heard 'em lighting off *fireworks.*

There another way out?
Um, sure.
You in some kind of trouble?
Not yet.
But Cleveland P.D. isn't big on asking questions first.
The Cleveland Preserver
Amen.
Goose it, you two.
We'll give 'em the runaround.
Glorious afternoon, officers!
Where'd you come from, anyway?
I heard a ***bang,*** and then you was just standing there, looking like you stepped out of the *Flash Gordon* funnies.
That's it.

That's *what?*
Do you know if *The Preserver* has started running a strip called, like, *Freddy Potato?*
Frankie Tomatah?
Yeah, it's two down from *Brick Bradford,* why?
I have to find the guy who draws it.
His *daughter,* more importantly.
Well, I doubt a guy that famous has got a listed number.
But I could maybe help you out...
...long as you give me those swell boots.

Are you fucking kidding me?
Stay back!
Lay a finger on me, I bring this *sap* down on your pretty--
NAH!
Hey!
You want a new pair of shoes, get back on your bike and sling papers.
But if I ever hear you tried to rob another kid, I'm going to find you and kick your teeth out of your face, understood?
Who... who *are* you?
Still figuring that out.

AAHHH!
...KJ...

I know you.

You're...you're the lady who invented **time travel.**
Haven't been called that in a long time.
Mac, isn't it?
But, I thought you and your friends all made it **home.**
When I finally got back to the late 21st century, the first thing I did was dig up what happened to... to each of you.
So you know **my** fairy tale ending, huh?
Yeah, first I heard it was gonna be leukemia, but according to a dickhole's second opinion, it's something called **4DC.**
Sweetheart, I'm so sorry.
I swear, I had no idea we'd have to pay so much for all this.
"We"?
They didn't realize when I was diagnosed either, but I'm Patient Zero of the same disease **you** regrettably contracted.
That's why I came here, to die with the rest of our planet.

Uh, about that second part...
In thirty-eight minutes, a gamma-ray burst from a nearby galaxy is going to permanently extinguish all life on Earth, just shy of her five billionth birthday.
And you came here by *choice?*
I didn't want Wari and Jahpo to have to deal with my ***remains,*** so when my health took a turn, I dug up my old Beta Model for one last trip.
Maybe it's cheating, but I thought it would be cool to hang on until the finish line, you know? To run the whole...
Forgive me, my manners are disappearing with the rest of my mind.
Qanta Braunstein, excellent-if-baffling to see you again.
Are you ***all right?*** How in the world did you end up ***here?***
I heard a strange noise--stranger than usual, anyway--and ran to investigate and... whatever, please, just tell me everything you can remember.
I kissed a girl.
Oh.

Tiffany Quilkin!
I've been waiting my whole life to meet you.

This is *your* fault!
RAHHHH!
Now just a--
Uhnf!
What did you do to my friends?!
That wasn't me!
It was one of my...my *predecessors!*
Bitch, what are you *talking* about?!

Please, just hear me out.
It was the *first* genetic duplicate of Erin Tieng who detonated the device that brought you here.
Her generation was a lot...angrier than mine.
Still, if it wasn't for those pioneers, we never would have ended the war.
The war...?
With the old-timers.
It's finally over.
Welcome to a harmonious utopia of complete global peace.
Can I get you some hot chocolate?

If your side were really the good guys, why did I just get ***blown up?***
You didn't.
You were safely transported thousands of years in your future. So you could ***help*** us.
Help you do what?
End the war, of course.
But, you just said--
Tiffany, we're the good guys because our side never stopped believing that a fairer, more just world was possible for everyone.
Unlike the old-timers, we still have hope.

We still have dreams.

CHAPTER 27

"Rule #4: A paperboy is always clean in appearance, dress and spirit."

–From *The American Newspaper Delivery Guild Handbook,* published in 1932

All clear.
It's safe for you to come out now.

About goddamn time.

You're a lifesaver, Charlotte.
Literary.
I think you mean "literally."
Sorry.
That's what I get for dropping Oldenglish my sophomore year.
Oh, Jude, are you sure you can't stay just a little longer?
I...I wish I could, but I have to get back to my friends, see if they've made any progress with our ship.
But you promise you'll let me see it? Your time machine?
Charlotte!
What the heck is wrong with the set?
The Real McCoys is about to start!
Uh-oh.

Go to your father, my dear.
I'll meet you back here tomorrow night.
You promise?
I swear.
The future still needs your help.
Hey, Jude.
VMMMMMMMM
Don't make it bad.

Yeah, I don't know what that means, but if you make any sudden moves, I'm gonna dropkick your face off.
You work for the old-timers?
Hardly.
I'm just a regular old ***kid*** trying to get home to 1988. That's where I met your buddies Heck and Naldo.
'88?
What the were we doing in that mess?
Beats me, but it started with you rolling my friend Tiffany for one of her pricey Radio Shack walkies.
Wait, not a TRC-218?
With channel 14 crystals?!
Huh?

My guys and I are like one of your old super-gods, ***Robyne Hude.***
We steal from the greedy past to give to our needy present, dig?
Whatever, can you get me back to my girlfriend or not?
Your...?
I mean, we're not "official" or anything.
But we probably will be, ***if*** you let me tag along.
Respect, kid.
I was still in the closet at your age, and my people actually ***like*** our kind.
Guess your era's way cooler than the history books say.

This hike... would be a lot easier...with a Camel Light... or twenty...
No time for vices, Mac.
We have to get you inside my capsule before ***the end.***
But, why can't you come ***with*** me?
Who says you have to die in some radioactive apocalypse with a bunch of disgusting monsters?
They're not monsters, they're the fittest survivors of billions of years of ***evolution,*** and some of the most beautiful creatures ever to walk our--
KAROOM

DOC!

My weapon!
Use it!

I'm trying!
Stupid thing's not working!
klik klik

iBeam!
Safety off, for Christ's sake!
Okay.
Hang on to your--
KRACK

UNF!
That was *hnn* badass.
You all right?
Sounded like you **broke** something.
Just my brother's old Walkman.
And the last thing I dubbed off him, probably.
Huh, my **father** used to have one much like this.
Your father?
Hey, why don't we just go back to **his** time, tell your younger self never to invent any of this crap?
I wish that were a possibility, but unfortunately, the world is like one of **these**.
A Prince-Sign O the Times
MEMOREX dBS 90

You lost me, Braunstein.
Time, it's not unlike your **cassette.**
It's comprised of one long spool, stretching from beginning to end, and each segment can only be recorded over so many times before it begins to **degrade.**
But, I'm not talking about erasing, like, all of human history!
Let's just go back and make sure that neither of us catch the shitty time-travel disease that's gonna do us both in!
I've tried, actually, but turns out that death is not unlike breaking the little **tab** off of one of these things.
Maybe it's God's way of making sure that His designs can only be changed so much.
Prince - Sign O the Times
Hold on.
You're saying God is **real?**
I know, when I was your age, I always **hated** when people ascribed whatever they didn't fully understand to some mythical being.
But the older I've gotten, the more I've come to believe that there must be **some** kind of higher power at work out there.
What kind of asshole creator would let a **kid** die?

You have every right to be pissed, Mac.
Nothing about life is fair...but at least yours isn't over yet.
So what? Even if I escape this nightmare, I have what, a few more years left, tops?
I know this will sound strange coming from someone in my line of work, but the amount of *time* we're each given is irrelevant.
It's what we choose to **do** with every second that counts.
Anyway, at least your tape survived.
Is it a good one?
Nah.
It's the fucking best.

What the eff is even happening right now?
Tiffany, this is my fellow genetic duplicate of Erin Tieng.
She's seven years older... if not always wiser.
Sup.
And you may recognize your friend **KJ** in this more distinguished clone of--
You.
You're... you're a copy of **me,** aren't you?
No, sweetheart.
I **am** you.

Say what now?
It's me, "Double-Oh Tiff"!
I'm the same older version of us you saved from my train wreck of a life back in 2000!
That... that isn't possible.
Hmmm, how can I prove it to you?
Well, remember third grade? When we shoplifted that pack of Garbage Pail Kids without getting caught? We've never confessed that to *anyone,* not even--
But, I watched you *explode!* And...and how you die is how you die!
True, but it only *looked* as if I perished.
Sixty years ago, people from this glorious paradise swooped in a split second before that blast to transport me to their time. They *Freejack-ed* me!
Who the hell is Free Jack?

Was that not out in '88?
Thought for sure I'd seen that when we were your age.
Tiffany, our foremothers rescued your older self for the same reason they gave birth to us: because you and each of your friends are vitally important to the future.
If that's true, where's ***Mac?***
Look, "it's complicated" is the understatement of the friggin' mega-annum.
But all you need to know is that these ladies and I are gonna reunite you with ***all three*** of your fellow papergirls.
Then why haven't you done it already?
Because we still need your assistance.
The only way our monstrous war--any war, really--finally ends is by opening up ***lines of communication.***

Back in the day, to talk across the ages, these folks would rely on coded letters left in newspapers by allies like the cartoonist woman you met.
But the old-timers eventually figured out that trick.
So we had to get a little more *creative* to send stuff they could never intercept.
Building off the brain-machine interface of ancient gadgets like this one, we invented a way to narrowcast transmissions directly into unconscious minds in the past.
Dreams.
Our dreams are secret messages from the *future.*
Told you I was a smart cookie.
But here's how it crumbles.
We've discovered that our creation works most clearly with one's ***contemporaries.***
All of us have tried talking to your pals, but not even Senior Citizen You can make a strong enough connection.
Which is where ***12-Year-Old You*** comes in.

You're the one person here who can break through to your crew.
We need you to reach out to as many as you can, and help guide them into position for a plan that will ultimately create peace on Earth.
This is totally bonkers.
What makes you guys think any of this is really going to work?
That's the thing, beautiful.
It already has.

Don't wuss out now, Erin.
The dream told you to moonwalk, right?
I think that means I have to *retrace my steps...*
...back to where this all started.
FORECLOSURE
FOR SALE

NO TRESPASSING!
BANK OWNED PROPERTY
direct call
Tiffany?
Anyone...?
Can't believe I'm doing this ***again.***
Um.
Hello?

Please.
I don't know what you want, but I'm just looking for something my friends and I found down here a few days...I mean, *years* ago.
Quit messing around.
I **know** this is where I'm supposed to be. I had, like, a...
...vision?
Yecch.
Boys are the *worst.*
Ahh!
RUV RUV RUUUVVV

God.
Oh, God.
You can do this, dummy.
Your family, your **friends,** everyone you love is on the other side of that thing.
It's like Mr. T says, "You gotta follow your dreams."
Just follow your...
NAIEEE!

OOHF!
Well.
Hey.

Awesome to finally make your acquaintance.

CHAPTER 28

"Rule #3: A paperboy sticks to his route, from start to finish."

–From *The American Newspaper Delivery Guild Handbook,* published in 1932

Why
are
we
here?

Now there's a question old as time.
I like to think it's *fate.*
Who gives a shit?
Philosophers don't last long in my line of work.
I was rather hoping *you* could tell us why we've ended up in this great beyond, Miss...?

No.
No way.
I don't have to tell you old-timers *anything.*

Believe it or not, Tiffany, "here" is actually your old neighborhood.
Though these days, it's way more ***Stream*** than Stony.
This entire sector frequently overlaps with the kind of fissures in four-dimensional space that allow us to ***communicate*** with other eras.
No offense, but that doesn't sound very ***scientific.***
Is fate really all that different than Einstein's determinism?
Sure, maybe you and your friends just ***happened*** to stumble onto that time machine, but I like to think the universe ***needed*** it to happen.
No, Jude, I mean, why did you drag me to ***Edgewater,*** where the acne crowd goes to lock braces?
Oh, when our "lifeboat" arrived in '58, it splashed down in your filthy lake, so my
and I set up camp not far from here.
Careful making your way down...
Grand Father, she's carrying the same satchel as the young ones who ***attacked*** *me in 001988!*
This poor girl's not our enemy, she's just an innocent bystander...isn't that right?

So wherever Erin, Mac, and KJ ended up, Old Sparky here is really going to let me *talk* to them? When they're ***asleep?***
And the message we need you to deliver is this: ***return to the beginning.***
Typically during their last period of R.E.M.
In the end, what's it matter?
Life existed on this rock for less than a blink of the universe's eye, and somehow, against truly astronomical odds, you and I both got to be part of it!
Man, for a terminal cancer patient, you're like a living Bobby McFerrin song.
Heck and Naldo are probably still out scavenging for parts, but they should be back soon.
Cool, it'd be good to see some familiar faces.
Yeah, you said you met the two of them...but what about ***me?***
Please, I just want to see my friends again.
And I give you my word we'll do everything in our power to make that happen.
For now, would you like to see our dinosaurs?

What does that *mean?*
At least one of your gal pals needs to find her way back to the same co-ordinates where you four first stumbled onto our forefathers' time machine.
But try to keep it simple. We've found that communiques sent this way tend to get a little ***Freddy Krueger-ed*** as they pass through the subconscious.
Afraid I don't understand the reference.
Right.
Before your time.
Uhhhhhm.
Save me the old "can't know your own future" speech, KJ!
If something awful is gonna happen to me, I deserve to hear about it!
Did you say...?
I gather you've been introduced to our teenaged opponents?
They've likely told you that we're terribly dogmatic about altering the past, but I assure you that's not the case.

I realize I'm biased, but why don't we start with Erin Tieng?
I'm trying, but nothing seems to be...
Just concentrate on her memory, and keep repeating the dispatch in your mind.
HNN.
Doc?
You okay?
I'm so sorry.
But I think you die.
Years ago, we learned you could rescue majestic creatures like these from moments before a comet strike, for example, and not alter the history of our planet one precious butterfly flap.
But our descendants have shown a reckless disregard for--
Sorry, do you feel that... tingling?

What the eff was that?!
Just a...a 4D **fault line** back to somewhere in the Paleocene Era, natural byproduct of this procedure.
Biggest one since our **first** test though.
Whatever, it means what you're doing is **working**, rockstar!
Go, Mac. Now. Do exactly what I told you.
But, it's too soon! I thought we still had a little more **time** before Earth was supposed to get microwaved or whatever!
This was... something else entirely.
Jude, are you all--
I'm gonna **die?**
In **this** lousy century?
Fuck.

But, we just accidentally blew chunks of the future into that time hole!
You *recognize* where it opened to, right?!
My girl.
I saw the place where I *found* her.
I wish there was something I could do, but...
Yeah, you can mess with time all you want, but there's no cheating death, huh?
Not like I was destined for a long life anyway.
I thought these monsters *worked* for you!
A few of the females left this realm to work *alongside* us...but I have no idea what these natives intend.
Regardless, I think we should get you *elsewhere.*

You've seen that place before?
I've **been** there!
You people... you must be who **Wari** thought was sending her stuff!
Her and her precious boy.
Oh.
Oh, Jesus.
You have the same disease as my...my girlfriend.
The one some **time travelers** get?
Most travelers by the time my generation rolls around. Lucky if you're immune. Our **implants** can redirect the mutations for a while...but nothing stops the inevitable.
Our four-dimensional guests first revealed themselves to the world when I was about your age, on the day we all discovered that time travel was possible.
What we call the **Editrixes** helped us understand the awesome responsibilities that come with--
Bullshit!

Sorry, who's Wari?
An old woman I met a...a long time ago.
No, she's a 12-year-old girl **we** met in exactly the past you guys have been dumping your mistakes into!
Tiffany, your older self doesn't remember any of your extra-temporal exploits before she encountered you as an adult in the year 2000.
Because all of this trauma will be **erased** before you and your friends are returned home safely.
I'd forgotten.
I'd forgotten how **beautiful** it was.
If time travel is pretty much a death sentence, why do you guys do it?
For all the kids who come **after** us.
And if there's some old piece of tech in your time that might help them down the line, then I...I know what I have to do.
Time travel wasn't "discovered," it was **invented...** by the woman who raised **you!**

What the hell did you just say?
Don't... be afraid.
It's not... as scary... as you think.
What isn't?
Do me a favor and don't tell my boyfriend what you know.
It's not like he could stop it, and I...I don't want him to be ***sad*** for however much time we've got left together.
What the hell did you just say?
That whatever war you've been part of is ***stupid.***
I barely understand it, but I still seem to know way more than ***you.***

Don't worry, whatever the old-timers are going to do to you-- to us--won't hurt a bit.
What do you mean going to do?! I thought all of this was about defeating the old-timers!
Actually, we told you we were going to end the war, not win it.
I promise... it doesn't even... hurt.
Almost feels... exciting?
Wow, you are so not like anyone I've ever met.
That's just the smell of a guy who hasn't bathed in literally decades.
Now let's move before the
strikes back.
Nothing you say makes a lick of sense.
My mother wasn't some inventor, she was--
AAAAHHH!

So my friends and I are getting our brains washed by the bad guys as part of your *surrender?*
This isn't a surrender, it's a *truce.*
One that will last *forever.*
...like something *wonderful...*
...is... about... to...
Come again?
I don't know how you'd translate it, but it's what we call that *blast* you saw back there.
Been happening more and more since we arrived, so just... try not to get killed by the next one, I guess.
CARDINAL!

My friends and I will forget everything that's happened! Everything that's *made* us friends!
I swear, it's a small price to pay for the lifetime of happiness you'll eventually find in this paradise.
You told me the next twelve years of my life will be a ***train wreck!*** Why do I have to make the same mistakes as you?!
Can I ask one last thing?
Do my boys at least get ***revenge*** on whatever asshole eventually does me in?
The old-timer who murders you, he...he gets ***shot.***
Don't shoot!
It's not trying to hurt her!
We don't know ***what*** it's doing!

It has to happen this way because it *did* happen this way.
I thought your side was the one that believed history could be *changed*. That if we had the power to go make things better, we *should*.
Now you sound like everything you used to fight *against*.
That's something, I guess.
Is it?
Aren't you sick of all this goddamn *death?*
I'm not losing anyone else!

I guess we *all* grow up to be old-timers, huh?
Spoken like a girl who's seen some shit.
I killed a man.
A *bad* man. In the past. The *way* past. I...I had to. To help save my friends.
BLAM

Um, guys?
Yo, Time Capsule!
Qanta Braunstein has added an authorized guest!
Welcome, authorized guest!
Yeah, that tracks.
As long as there have been young people, there have been older ones forcing us to fight their--
Um, Jude?

Is it finally happening?
Yep.
The last domino's been tipped.
Destination?
Back home.
Ass-crack of the morning on November 1, 1988.
EMERGENCY LAUNCH
OVERRIDE
AFETY PROTOCOLS
00:03
Oh...

NOOOoo!
It's a trap!
Make it snappy.
KJ, don't!
It's all right.
I've seen this before.
...crap.

CHAPTER 29

"Rule #2: A paperboy smokes neither cigarillo nor pipe 'til his work is done."

–From *The American Newspaper Delivery Guild Handbook,* published in 1932

Warning: AppleX User Terms and Conditions have been updated.

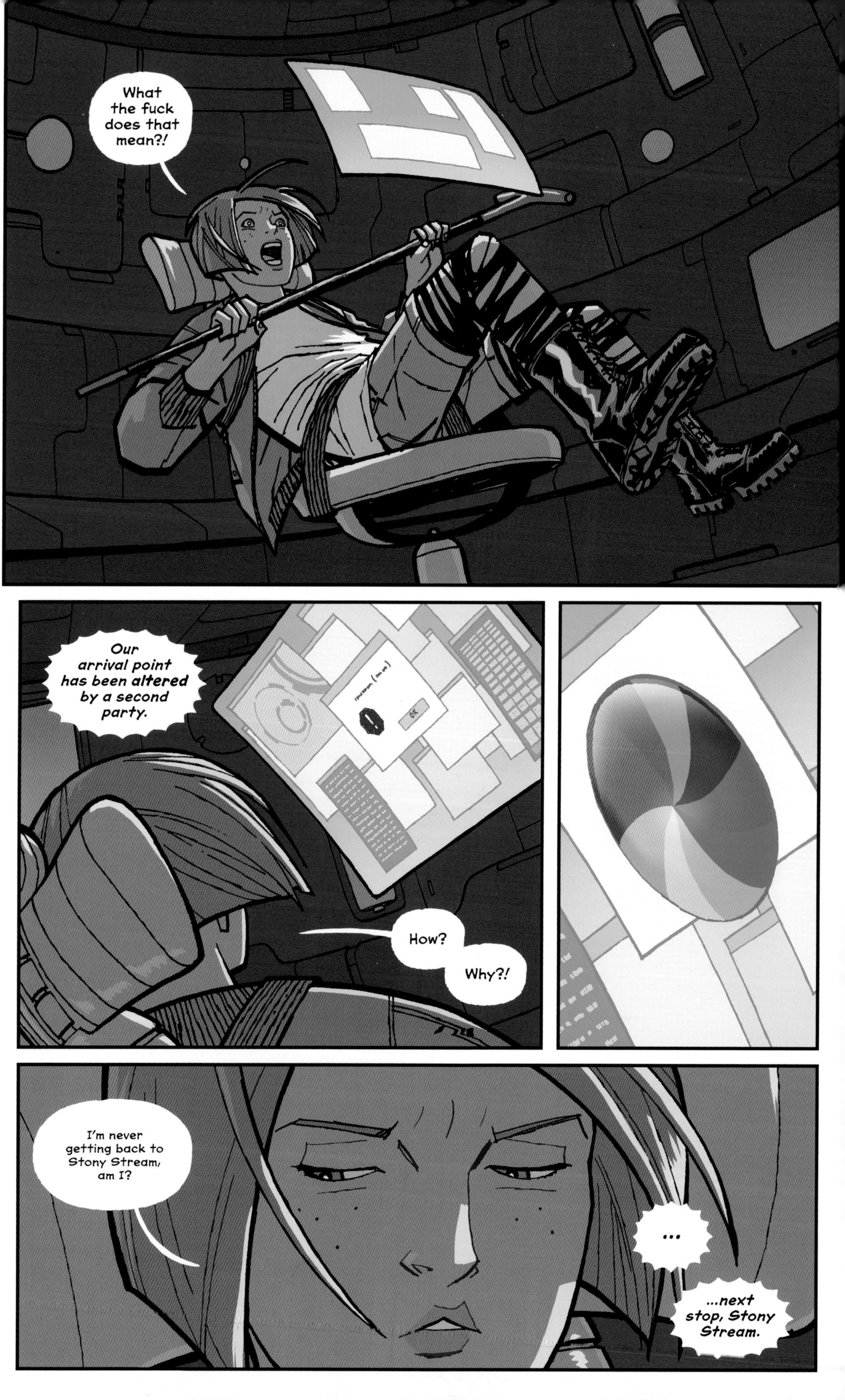
What the fuck does that mean?!
Our arrival point has been altered by a second party.
How?
Why?!
I'm never getting back to Stony Stream, am I?
...
...next stop, Stony Stream.

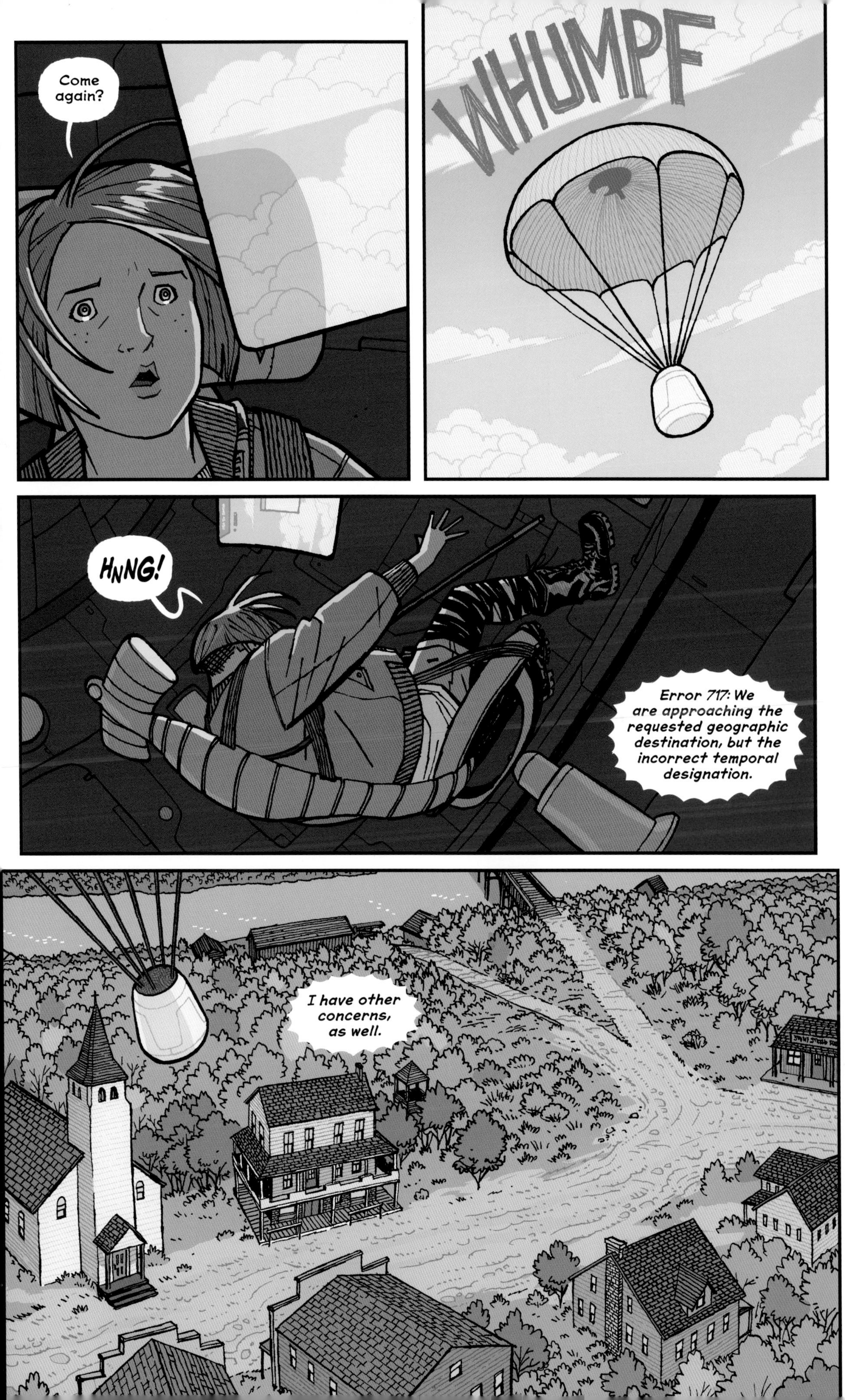
Come again?
WHUMPF
HNNG!
Error 717: We are approaching the requested geographic destination, but the incorrect temporal designation.
I have other concerns, as well.

Time Capsule, what year is this?
Are there gonna be goddamn dinosaurs when I step out there?
Today is Tuesday, August 2, 1831.
But although it is approaching noon, HealthX readings suggest that all inhabitants of this hamlet are asleep.
FSSSS.
Well, that makes absolutely no sense.

Whatever, how long will it take to get to 1988 from here?
It will take... sorry, remaining battery is reserved for Doctor Braunstein's Last Will & Testament.
Confirmed, delivering to primary beneficiary.
Please stand clear of the closing door.
Hey, no, what are you--
Thank goodness you made it, Mac.

If your bad ass hadn't survived to join us, the entire third dimension would have *shattered* like a...a...
...what do you call the top of a crème brûlée?
What the hell is happening?
Is this a dream?
Nope, that future version of me is *real.*
The bad news is, she and her weird buddies want to *lobotomize* us.
Tiffany!
You're not dead yet!

My team and I didn't come to this neutral ground to **hurt** anyone, but to safely transport you to the same predawn hours of November from which you disappeared.
We just need to...**adjust some memories** before sending you home.
And for what it's worth, just because you'll forget a few days together doesn't mean your experiences didn't really happen.
Which means I'm still going to **bite it,** yeah?
Figured.
It's not fair!
If you've got this higher-than-high tech, why don't we go **way** back, stop us from ever finding that stupid time machine in the first place?
We tried, actually.
Millions and millions of times.

In every attempt to retcon that stretch of the timestream, the best we could ever do was, like, change the date Mac first met another one of you girls by a few weeks.
The "current" is now so strong at that point in the "stream," it's all but impossible for you four not to be drawn together into that dank Ohio basement.
That's almost worse than never meeting at all! If all we remember is delivering a few papers, we won't stay together.
You said it yourself, the four of us drift apart after that last Hell Morning.
You've learned what Newton said about every action, right?
Besides, you're twelve.
No matter what happens next, you'll make plenty of new--
How did I not notice it?
You're...you're her, aren't you? Only, old and stuff?
Not exactly, Ms. Coyle.
I'm but a humble, 42-year-old clone of your friend KJ, created to weather the same kinds of storms as the original article.
Who, by the by, should be joining us in three...two...

...hello?
Kaje!
Careful.
How can we be sure this isn't another evil mimeograph of her?
Because I know you taste like cigarettes and Ultra Brite toothpaste.
...is that bad?
It's memorable.

What is *wrong* with you kids?
Can't you leave anything well enough alone?!

He's got Erin!
GUN!
Steady on, Old-Timer.
We come in peace...
...but we didn't come *unarmed.*
Peace?
You blew up our Cathedral, killed every last soul aboard!
Actually, *your* actions caused the ship's destruction, but before your people could perish, *we* safely transported all of them back where they belong.
Then why haven't you let us to do the same for *this* girl?!
If she and her companions aren't deposited back in their era shortly, all of space and time will fracture like...like...
Yeah, crème brûlée, we heard.
And we know what needs to be done, Grand Father.
But first, we need something from *you.*

We're not just papergirls, we're friends.
The heck do you keep saying, Tiff?
A Hail Mary?
Kind of.
*We're not just papergirls, we're **friends**.*
We're not just papergirls...
Whatever it is, ***no***.
After all the friends I lost on C-Day, I won't negotiate with terrorists, not even when the very continuum is on the line.

This isn't a negotiation, it's a ***blood oath.***
If your generation will agree to the immediate and permanent cessation of ***all*** nonstandard movement through four-dimensional space...then so will ours.
But.
You're talking about the end of time travel.
Forever and ever, amen.
Obviously, we can't prevent whatever excursions have ***already*** taken place along the line, but together, we can ensure that this power is never exploited again.
Listen to her!
Don't you want this stupid war to ***end?***
I do.
Which is why I've fallen for empty gestures from our descendants before.
I'm sorry.

So are we.
Because we didn't just pluck *you* from the next dimension over.
eh?

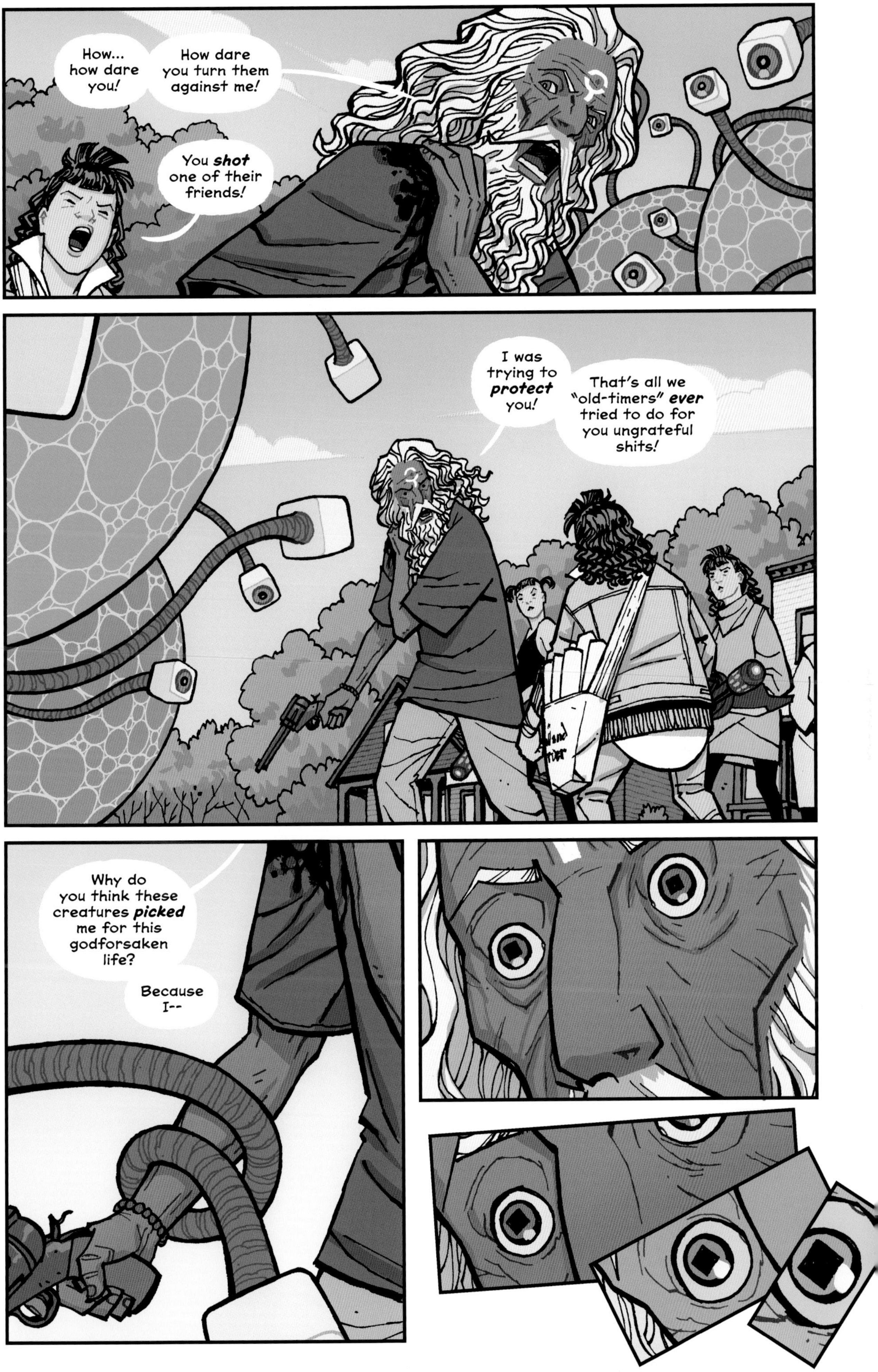

How... how dare you!
How dare you turn them against me!
You **shot** one of their friends!
I was trying to **protect** you!
That's all we "old-timers" **ever** tried to do for you ungrateful shits!
Why do you think these creatures **picked** me for this godforsaken life?
Because I--

WATCH
NEEDZ U!
NG GORENG

I'll be damned.
I am...
...not the man I thought I was.
The Stones were wrong.
Time isn't on *anyone's* side, is it?
For what it's worth, took *us* thousands of years to finally learn that lesson.
Hhn.
Your terms.
I *agree.*

That's it?
No epic final battle?
Can you please sound less disappointed?
Does that mean we get to go home?
You'll each be safely deposited back in your lives, in the early hours shortly *after* you originally found the time machine, events you'll no longer recall.
I vaguely remember waking up *late* for my route that day, which I blamed on some crazy-vivid nightmares I instantly forgot.
I know it sounds like a lot, but removing all of the trauma you were exposed to is actually the *least* we can do.
Trauma? This has been the best time of my life!
I *rode* a gigantic microscopic bug! Like at a *rodeo!*
Yeah, why can't we just hold onto the good stuff?
Like my cool new boots.
I hate you.

Unfortunately, this is a package deal.
Anything you picked up during your travels has to stay behind, including what's in here.
It's for the best, girls.
One of you *took a life*, and while that may not weigh on her yet, I promise it would over time.
She'd come to dwell not just on the man she was forced to end, but on all of the *descendants* she likely helped erase from history.
Believe me, endless branches of their possible faces will haunt her for the rest of--
Enough!
I vote we get on with the brainwashing already.

Mac, are you sure?
No.
But at least I'll go back to not really believing that I'm gonna *die* someday.
That'll feel nice, right?
And who knows?
Even if the four of us are destined to lose touch, at least we'll have--
Apologies, but time is of the essence.

I...I didn't even get to say *goodbye!*
And all that pain you're feeling is about to disappear, too.
We're not just papergirls, we're--
WAIT!
What Eve did!
In the Garden of Eden!
I...I don't think it was *evil.*

It was smart.
It was *right.*
Does anyone know what the hell she's talking about?
The mythical first woman.
From their Bible?
Don't worry, beautiful.
That's just another silly old story...
...written by a bunch of dudes.

CHAPTER 30

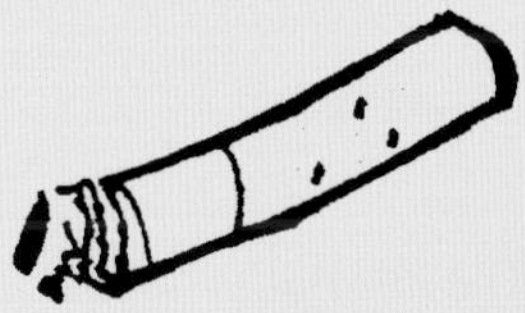

RIP

"Rule #1: A paperboy treats every other paperboy as his brother."

–From *The American Newspaper Delivery Guild Handbook,* published in 1932

If you laugh at me, I'm gonna punch you in the boob.
KJ
Karina

Jesus.
Pretty much the opposite.
KJ, you look...
I mean, I didn't know this was gonna be so... dressy.
Relax, it's not *your* bat mitzvah.
Am I the only kid not from your school here?
Sorry I'm late!

This stupid thing got stuck in my **spokes.**
New kid!
Mac, you've known me for almost a **year.**
How come you don't just call me by my real name?
Because I...I have no idea what it is.
Neither do I, actually.
When did we meet again?
You guys, listen to me.
It's super, super important that you **don't forget** what I'm about to--
GUN!

Hey.
Y LOGGING:
5 65311
9 10930
75 76 75744
65 21 12025
53 78 10690
Tiff?
What are you--
RRIDE MULTIPLE TARGETS
SSESSMENT: POTENTIAL DO
EMBER NUMBER: 3905137
See you real soon.
ERIN!
snap
That was her name.

I have a message.
Please.
You have to dance with me.
Like, *slow* dance?
Remember.
We're not just papergirls. We're--
Mac, you *love* me.
I do?
I--
DUDE!

Mmf?
You overslept, stupid.
...time is it?
Like, five something.
NO PARKING ANY TIME
Oh, shit.
It's Hell Morning.
And my boys are still out there, so I hope you're ready to get egged in the *face*.

Is Dad home yet?
I doubt it.
Why?
'Cause I could use a hand rubber-banding my stack.
Don't look at me.
Ain't my route anymore.
Cool jacket, butch.
Goddammit.
What now?
I can't fall asleep without James and Lars!
Where the hell's my Walkman?
Beats me.

WOMEN
for
BUSH
88

Karina?

Aren't you late for your little job, sweetheart?
Oh.
Yeah, thanks, Mom.
I would have woken you up sooner, but it looked like you were having the sweetest dream of all time.
I kind of was, actually.
It was sometime in the *future,* and my friends and I were all at this amazing party, and... and...
...shoot.
It's gone.

PRESS START TO CONTINUE
...not... just... paper...
...ghuh?
SS1101
SS1101
PRESS START TO CONTINUE
ROUND 36
36
Holy cow.
I'm at *the end.*

Round 36.
Another fifteen minutes, and I could probably **beat** it, or at least figure out a way to...
ARKANOID
ROUND 36
What is **wrong** with you?
ESS START
CONTINUE
ROUND 36
Nintendo
ENTERTAINMENT SYSTEM
POWER
RESET

KERRASH
The heck?
Sorry, Missy.
My alarm must not have gone off, and if I don't hurry--
What's on your stomach?
MONSTER SQUAD
My...?

Huh.
Erin, did you get a *tattoo?*
It's not a tattoo, it's more like a... *rash.*
I've never seen one like *that.*
Yeah, well, you don't even know what puberty is.
All sorts of weird stuff starts happening to your--
I'm telling Mom.
Missy, please.
If you do that, she's not going to let me make my rounds, and the *Preserver* will *fire* me.
So what? It's not like you have to pay for your own food or clothes or anything! Why do you need this so bad?
You'll understand when you're older.

Mac!
How's it going?
Say again?
Don't know if you remember, but we delivered together last year.
Tonya, right?
Tiffany.
Anyway, the psychos are still out in full effect. You want to team up again?
Maybe.
Have you, *uh,* seen **KJ** tonight?
CAMEL LIGHTS

Not yet.
But I ran into some new deliverer named Erin.
Is he a dork?
She seemed all right to me.
Erin with an "E"? For real?
How many of us are working Stony Stream now?
Guess you started a fad.
Hnn.
Where's the new kid now?
Over in the evergreen streets.
Told her to give me a call if anything comes up.
Give you a call ***how?*** The nearest payphone is like a ***mile*** from here.
Welcome to the future.
The Cleveland Preserver

A walkie-talkie?
Hardly.
This is a Realistic TRC-218 CB with channel--
≶kzzt≷ Um, calling Tiffany? ≶kzzt≷
It's me, the girl you gave this thing to? Um, over? ≶kzzt≷
Definitely a dork.
What's up, Erin?
I don't know yet, exactly. I...I didn't know if I should follow them by myself or what.
But I saw three creepy guys in costumes follow ***another*** papergirl down that cul-de-sac at the end of Hemlock...and she hasn't come out yet.
Over.

Get away from me.
Relax, we just wanted to meet the new chick.
Yeah, I didn't recognize those legs.
You go to St. Nick's or St. Pete's?
Neither.
I'm...I'm at Buttonwood.
Thought I smelled academy.
Tell me something.
Is it true what they say about Jewish girls?
Lucas Kurzenberger!

Cool costume, you...
...you...

...fart-mouth.
What did you just call me?
Trust me, she's said way worse.
And she's not wrong.
Yeah, a little Listermint wouldn't kill you.
Why don't you mind your business, Coyle?
That's exactly what I'm doing, unlike *your* unemployed ass.
My brother told me you got fired from Friendly's for dipping your hairy balls in the Fribble machine.
Hffh.
Ha ha.
Good luck getting home alive, bitch.

I could have handled them on my own, you know.
You're welcome?
KJ, this is Erin.
It's great to meet you, *all* of you. I just wanted to say, I'm so impressed by--
There are more of those dipshits out there.
We should keep moving.
I was thinking we could split up into two groups, finish the development faster?
Or?
Because of the evil high schoolers and stuff?
Maybe all four us could maybe...stick together?
Just an idea.

ARRRRRR OOOOOOOO
RROOOO
What's with these dweebs?
I outgrew trick-or-treating when I was *eight.*
Who'd you go as, Tiff?
I don't know, either an astronaut or the devil.
How about you guys?

Probably Annie.
I was *obsessed* with that movie when it came out.
Yeah, I dressed up as Miss Hannigan that year.
The bad guy?!
But, you didn't even need a wig to be the hero!
Annie is fine and all, but Hannigan is a total *badass.* There's a *reason* she gets invited to the White House at the end of the...
Whatever, it's stupid.
Back in '83, I dressed up as Robin. From Batman? But I got scared looking out my window at all the neighborhood kids and went to hide under my parents' bed.
I ended up getting a fever and didn't go out, and that was pretty much it for my mom and dad, so I never went out on Halloween again.
That is the single saddest story I've heard in my entire life.
HONK HONK

Go around, asshole!
Ah, man.
Not the station wagon again.

This guy has bothered you before?
Lady, actually.
A few days ago, I think she tried *following* me, and I had to--
STOP
SCREE

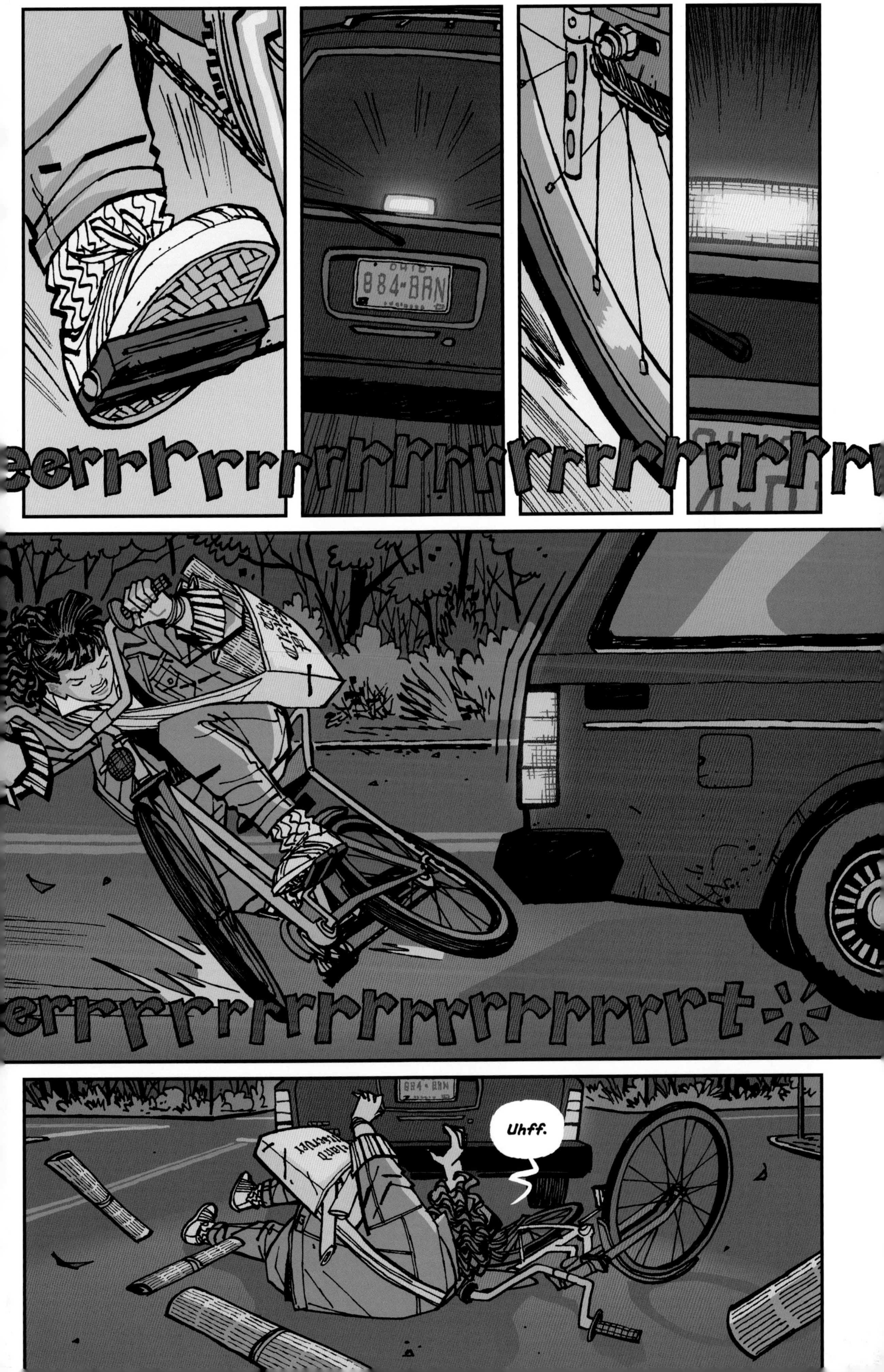

OHIO
884-BRN
Uhff.

Are you all right?!
What the hell, lady?!
You could have--

OHIO
254-AXY
CUYAHOGA

Eff me.
If...if we had crossed that intersection...
STOP
STOP
VRRRRRRRRRRRRR
WAIT!
Who are you?!

What's it matter?
I'm just glad the drunk idiot almost hit us when she did.
But, what if it ***wasn't*** an accident?
What if that was, like... our guardian angel?
flic
You know *Highway to Heaven* is fake, right?
Ah, Mac.
May I have a cigarette?
Please...?

Hhhh.
With all the warnings and stuff, I didn't think it was gonna *taste* so great.
Good ol' forbidden fruit.
≷koff≶
But, aren't you worried about *dying?*
Not as worried as I am about living a life that isn't fuckin' awesome.
I think I'm going to quit.
You only started three puffs ago!
Not smoking, *delivering.*
I'm pretty sure my papergirl days are done.

Why, Tiffany?
Don't get me wrong, I loved this job.
I never thought I'd be able to knock on complete strangers' doors and tell them to pay me. And I started doing that shit when I was eleven years old!
But these days, it's kind of become only about the money.
And what's wrong with that?
Hey, I've been able to buy myself more stuff than I ever could have imagined... but it's still stuff.
And most of whatever I think I'll like is just some slightly different version of crap that made me feel happy when I was a kid.
I mean, maybe I need to grow up a little?
So quitting a paying job is more "grown up" than having one?
Yeah, what are you ever gonna do that will be better than this?
I don't want to do anything, I just want to...be.
At least for a little while.

And you know when your last morning will be and every-thing?
I was kind of thinking I'd turn my bag over to the *Preserver* **today.**
If you three would be willing to pick up my customers?
Jackpot.
Yeah, thank you so much.
But, don't you still have a few last porches left?
Down to my final four.
Then let's get to it.
I mean, our handbook clearly says, "A paperboy always finishes strong."
Have you looked around?
Paperboys went extinct.
tssssssss

WHAPF
Can't believe you're *retiring* that beautiful arm.
I'm serious, you should really think about lacrosse.
Heh, maybe.
Is that the goddamn sun coming out already?
Stupid day-light savings, messes me up every year.
I don't know, I kind of *like* it.
Especially in the fall, when we get a whole extra hour.
Sometimes, I'll stay awake until three in the morning, just so I can, you know, experience those same sixty minutes *twice.*
Why?
...
I have no idea.

Well.
This has been real, but I should be getting home.
Same here.
Maybe we'll do this again next year, new kid.
Yeah, maybe so.
And I'll probably still see you around the neighborhood, right?
Almost definitely.
Okay then.
Catch you freaks later.

Later.
See ya!
Bye.

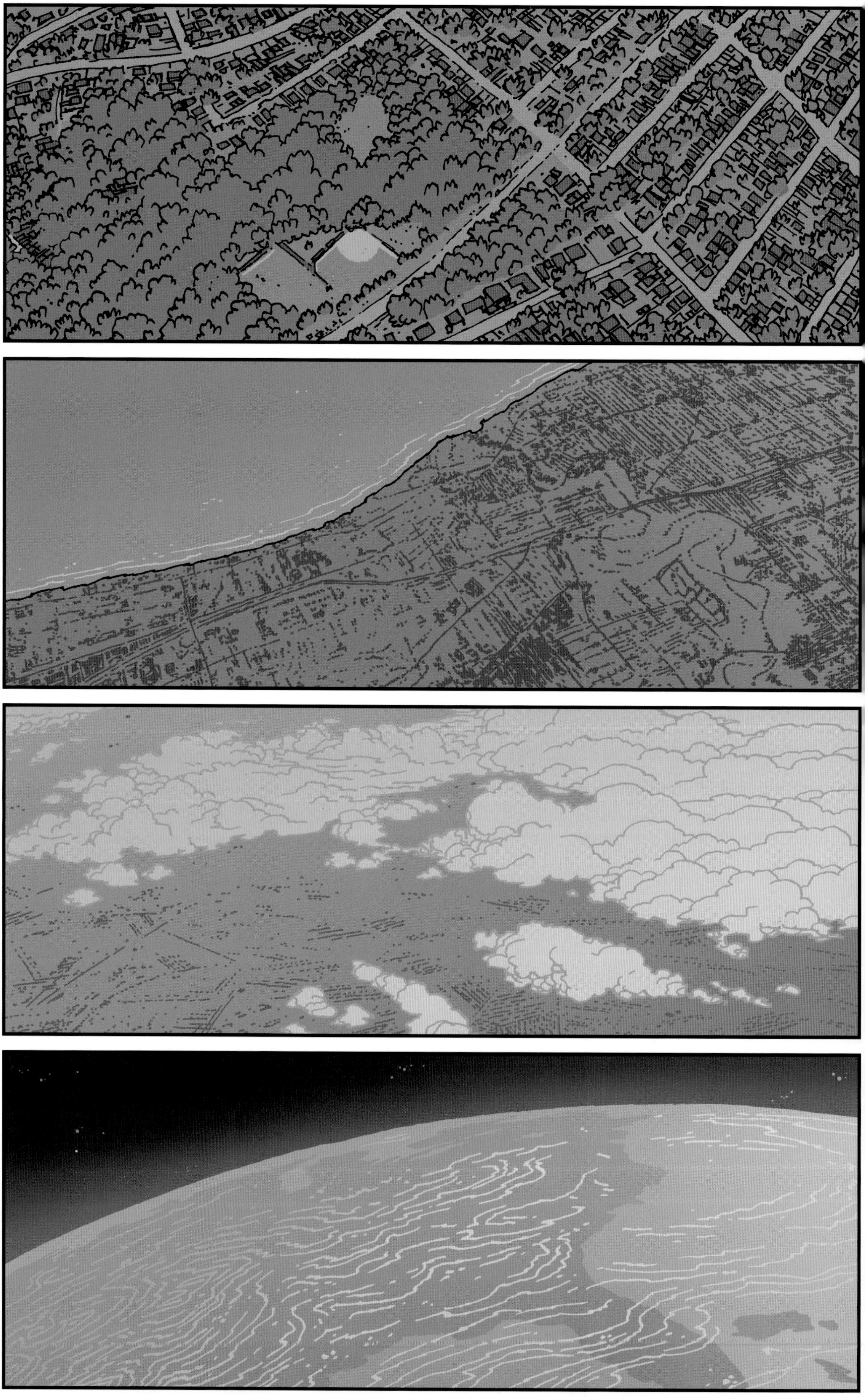

Wait!

You guys!
Hold up!
Hey.
Um, I'm not sure about you, but I don't have to start getting ready for school for, like, another hour.
Want to ride together a little longer?

...sure.
Why not?
Yeah, I'm in.
Cool.
fump
Ow.
What was that for?
Yellow punch buggy.

No punch backs.

ART Gallery

Above: bind-in posters from single issues

Below: cover sketches for Paper Girls vol. 1 *and 2, and color tests for later volumes*

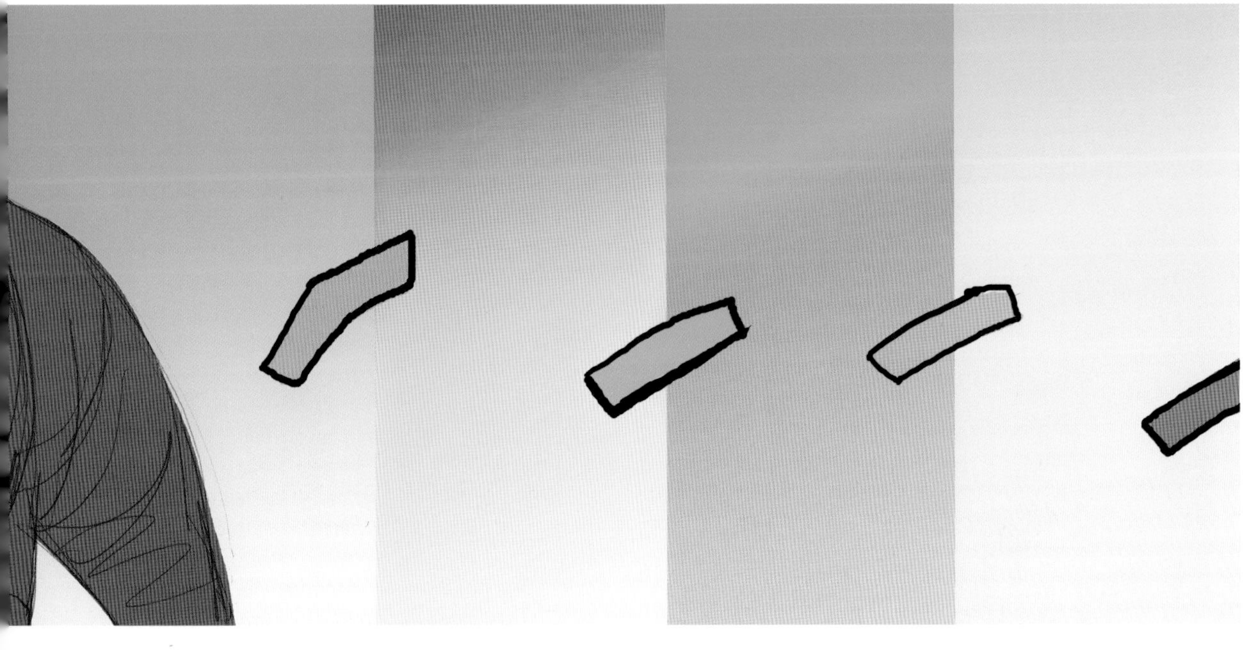

Brian K. Vaughan, #1 *New York Times* bestselling writer of *SAGA*, and **Cliff Chiang,** legendary artist of *WONDER WOMAN*, return with acclaimed colorist **Matt Wilson** and innovative letterer **Jared K. Fletcher** for the second volume of *PAPER GIRLS*, as the hit series continues with a bold new direction.
After surviving the strangest night of their lives in the Cleveland suburb of Stony Stream, intrepid young newspaper deliverers Erin, Mac and Tiffany find themselves launched from 1988 to a distant and terrifying future...the year 2016.
What would you do if you were suddenly confronted by your 12-year-old self? 40-year-old newspaper reporter Erin Tieng is about to find out in this action-packed story about identity, mortality, and growing older in the 21st century.
"You should all be reading Brian K. Vaughan and Cliff Chiang's comic series now." —The Los Angeles Times
"The feminist comic series for fans of Stranger Things." —The Huffington Post
"Paper Girls tells its story from the point of view of young women, not boys, and it doesn't seem coincidental that its tone is harder, flintier, funnier, more pragmatic, and far less concerned with idealizing the 'lost innocence of childhood.'" —NPR
"The book has a lot going for it, but Matt Wilson's color work is reason enough to be interested." —Comics Bulletin
BRIAN K. VAUGHAN
CLIFF CHIANG
MATT WILSON
JARED K. FLETCHER
VOL 03 | $12.99
IMAGECOMICS.COM
image
PAPER GIRLS
VAUGHAN CHIANG WILSON FLETCHER
3
Paper Girls
3

Paper Girls
4

Paper Girls
5

Paper Girls
6

Paper Girls
21

Paper Girls
22

6' 0"
5' 6"
5' 0"
4' 6"
4' 0"
3' 6"
3' 0"
Paper Girls
23

Paper Girls
24

Paper Girls
25

Paper Girls
26
RIP

Paper Girls
27

Paper Girls
28

Paper Girls
29

Paper Girls
30

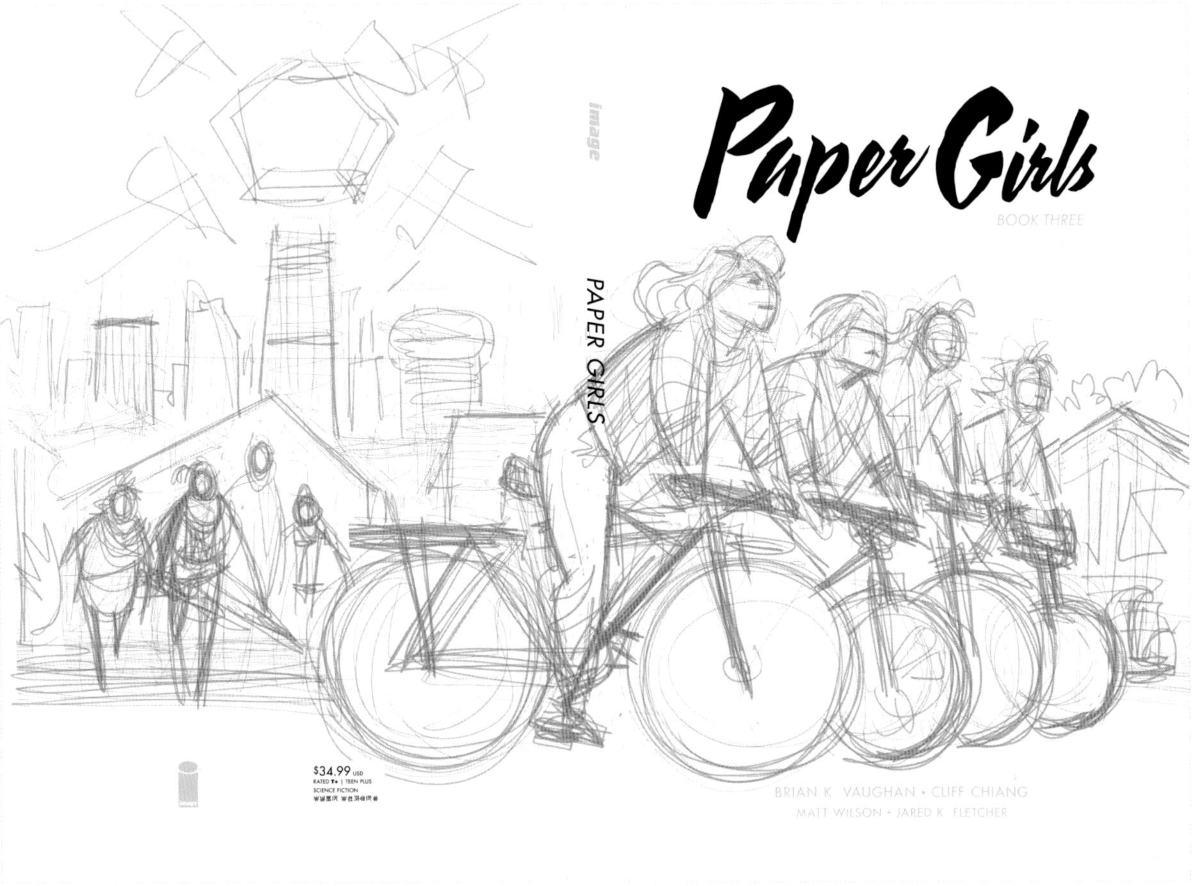

Cover sketch for Paper Girls Deluxe Book 3

A.N.D.G. postcard, lineart from a signing at Austin Books & Comics

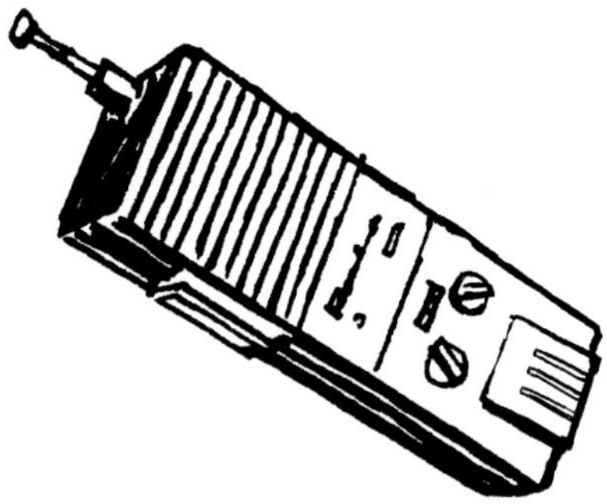

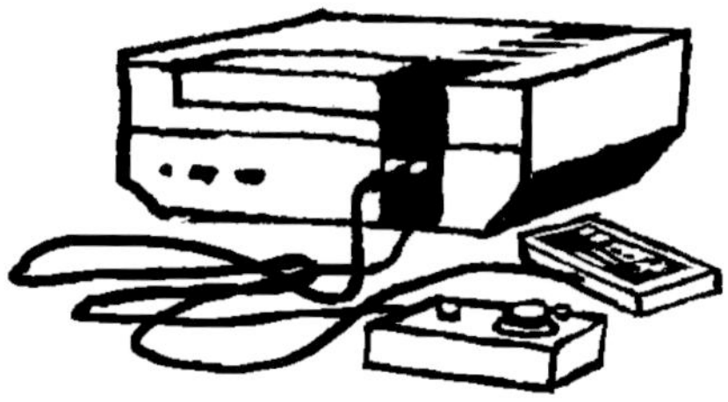

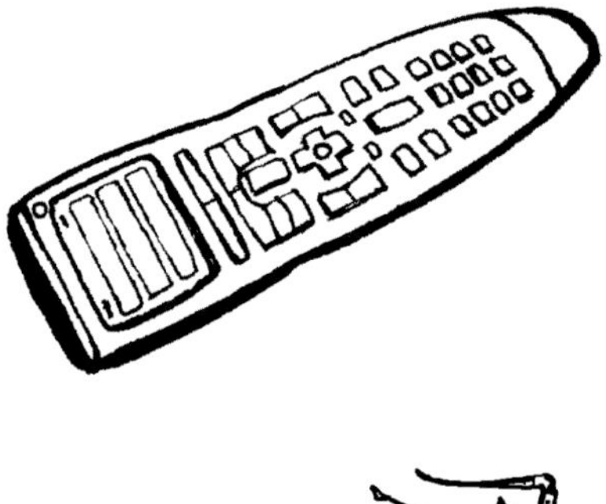

Letter column and "Next Issue" vignette art

4TH FOLDING NOW
TURKISH & DOMESTIC BLEND
CAMEL
LIGHTS
DON'T TRUST OTHER ERIN!!!

New YEAR

APPLE PIE
A Prince-Sign O the Times
MEMOREX

Above, and following pages: A.N.D.G. letter column mascots

RITA'S
DELIVERY
BAG

RITA'S
DELIVERY
BAG

Petey Roy & Rita Pearl enamel pin set

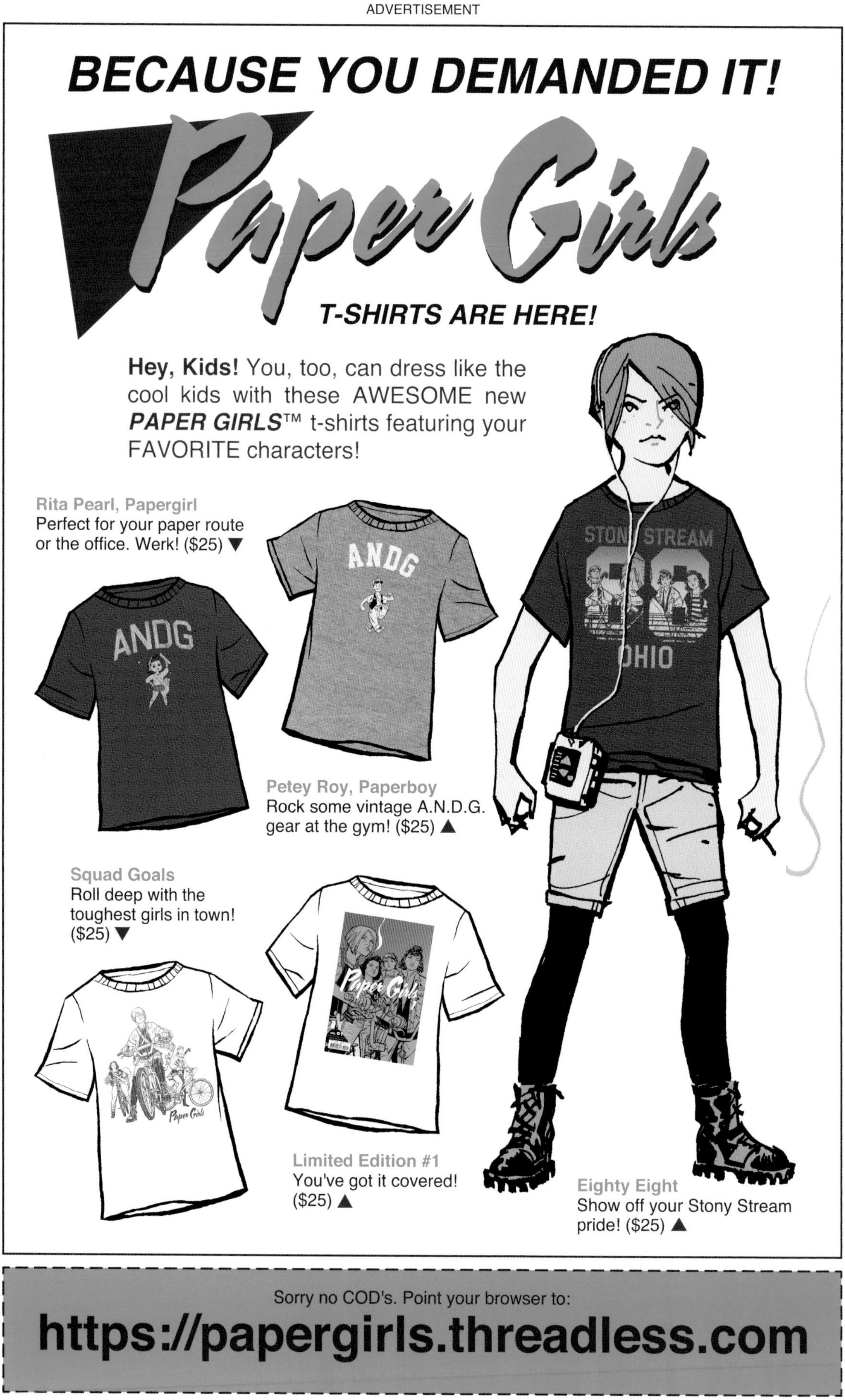
ADVERTISEMENT
BECAUSE YOU DEMANDED IT!
Paper Girls
T-SHIRTS ARE HERE!
Hey, Kids! You, too, can dress like the cool kids with these AWESOME new PAPER GIRLS™ t-shirts featuring your FAVORITE characters!
Rita Pearl, Papergirl
Perfect for your paper route or the office. Werk! ($25) ▼
ANDG
ANDG
Petey Roy, Paperboy
Rock some vintage A.N.D.G. gear at the gym! ($25) ▲
OHIO
Squad Goals
Roll deep with the toughest girls in town! ($25) ▼
Paper Girls
Limited Edition #1
You've got it covered! ($25) ▲
Eighty Eight
Show off your Stony Stream pride! ($25) ▲
Sorry no COD's. Point your browser to:
https://papergirls.threadless.com

House ads for Paper Girls t-shirts

ADVERTISEMENT

BECAUSE YOU DEMANDED IT!
Paper Girls
T-SHIRTS ARE HERE!
NEW DESIGNS!
Hey, Kids! You, too, can dress like the cool kids with these AWESOME new PAPER GIRLS ™ t-shirts featuring your FAVORITE characters!
SPORTS
*Batteries not included. ($25) ▼
SPORTS
TO BE CONTINUED
TO BE CONTINUED
Rock 'em, sock 'em! ($25) ▲
Paper Girls
WORLD TOUR 1988
SUNRISE
Hang ten, dude! ($25) ▼
Paper Girls
andg
Y2K
Only shooting stars break the mold ($25) ▲
WORLD TOUR
You will, you will, rock us! ($25) ▲
Sorry no COD's. Point your browser to:
https://papergirls.threadless.com

ADVERTISEMENT

BECAUSE YOU DEMANDED IT!
Paper Girls
T-SHIRTS ARE HERE!
NEW DESIGNS!
Hey, Kids! You, too, can dress like the cool kids with these AWESOME new PAPER GIRLS ™ t-shirts featuring your FAVORITE characters!
RUNNING UP THAT HILL
There is thunder in our hearts. ($25)
EYES FRONT
Take point with Wari, everyone's favorite Jurassic teen mom. ($25)
ANDG
MECHA ME CRAZY
You Are (Not) Alone ($25)
ANDG 3000
Ain't nobody dope as Dash-Dash-Dot the Paperbot. So fresh and so clean! ($25)
Rita Pearl, Papergirl
Perfect for your paper route or the office. Werk! ($25)
Sorry no COD's. Point your browser to:
https://papergirls.threadless.com

DESIGN PROCESS

Gallery

From cover to cover, Paper Girls *has a unique look thanks to its strong graphic design. Whether it's the bold and evocative book logo, the colorful yet minimalist title pages, or the warmth of the word balloons and lettering, designer Jared K. Fletcher strikes a delicate balance between a knowing '80s nostalgia and a clean, modern appeal. He's created logos for* The X-Men, Wonder Woman, Spider-Gwen, *and most recently, the first three waves of books from* TKO Studios *(which includes a stunning, unified package design). Here, Jared gives us a behind-the-scenes look at his process and some of the artistic choices that go into the lettering and design of* Paper Girls.

Alien font decoded!

When Cliff told me we would need an "alien" font in the comic, I initially suggested that we should review some of the great alien-looking comic fonts available and pick one. I have a few in my lettering toolbox that I often go to for similar cases, and usually it's just gibberish text for a few balloons and nothing too complicated. However, Cliff wanted to build something new for this book from the ground up. Brian was going to write actual dialogue for these characters, and the font could serve as cipher code for their language. So I set to work designing a font for a language for aliens who, as I would later discover, were in fact teenagers from the future.

Cliff suggested using the Korean alphabet as a starting point. I did some research and built out a big digital spread of different Hangul characters that I thought looked interesting. On another layer, I began sketching in my own version of these letterforms. I liked the clean uniformity of the strokes. Incorporating the dot added an "alien" element that unified the letters and created a unique font. The first pass had a little over two hundred different letterforms.

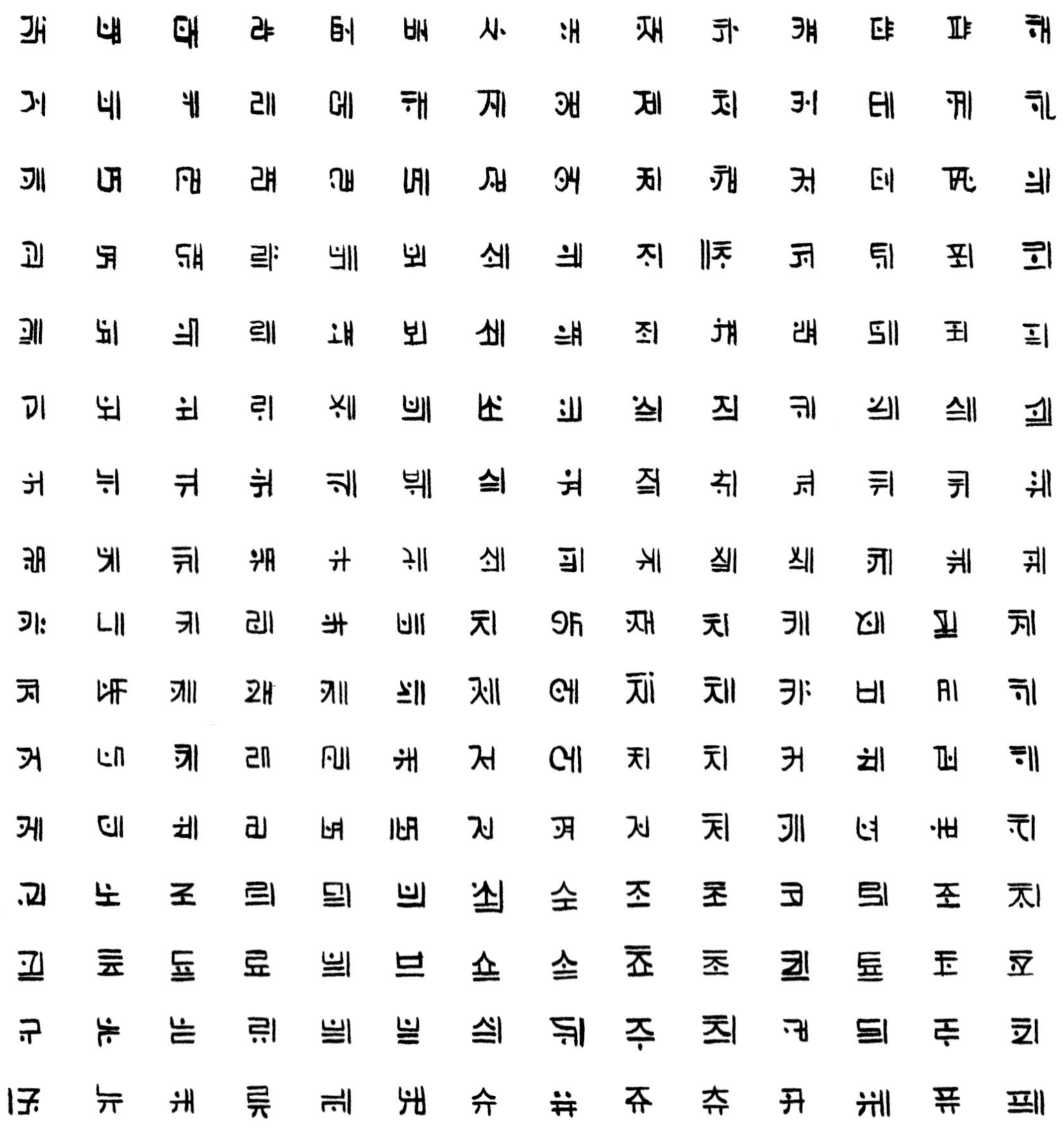

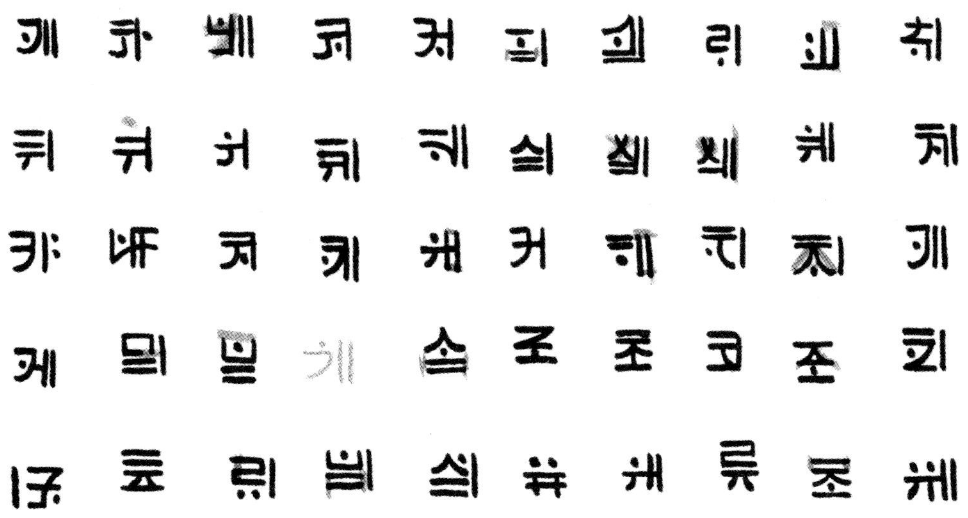

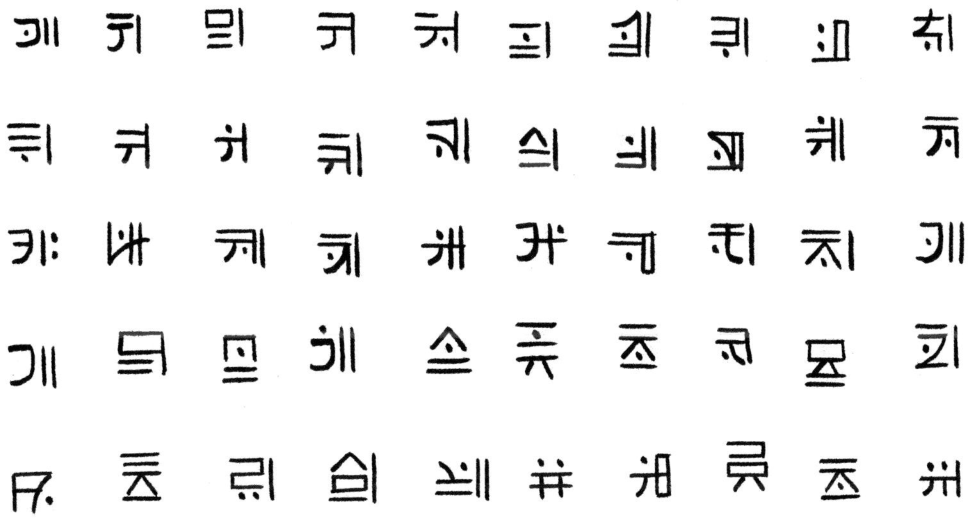

The first large batch looked too recognizably Korean, and Cliff wanted me to push the letterforms further to create my own design. I picked fifty of the characters I liked most from the first batch and used them as the basis for another layer. I did that two more times, refining and making every letterform more legible with each new phase of the design. Once I felt that each letterform was unique and stood on its own, I whittled down the set to the final thirty letterforms we ended up using.

At this stage, I planned to ink these letters by hand in Adobe Photoshop and convert them to vector shapes to be exported as a font set. However, I didn't like how organic these shapes turned out in my digital inks, so I changed course and built the letterforms using vectors instead. Ultimately, I wanted to be able to control how thick the line weights were in the letters. Deciding to use vectors allowed me to use the pen tools in Adobe Illustrator and gave me a lot of freedom to experiment.

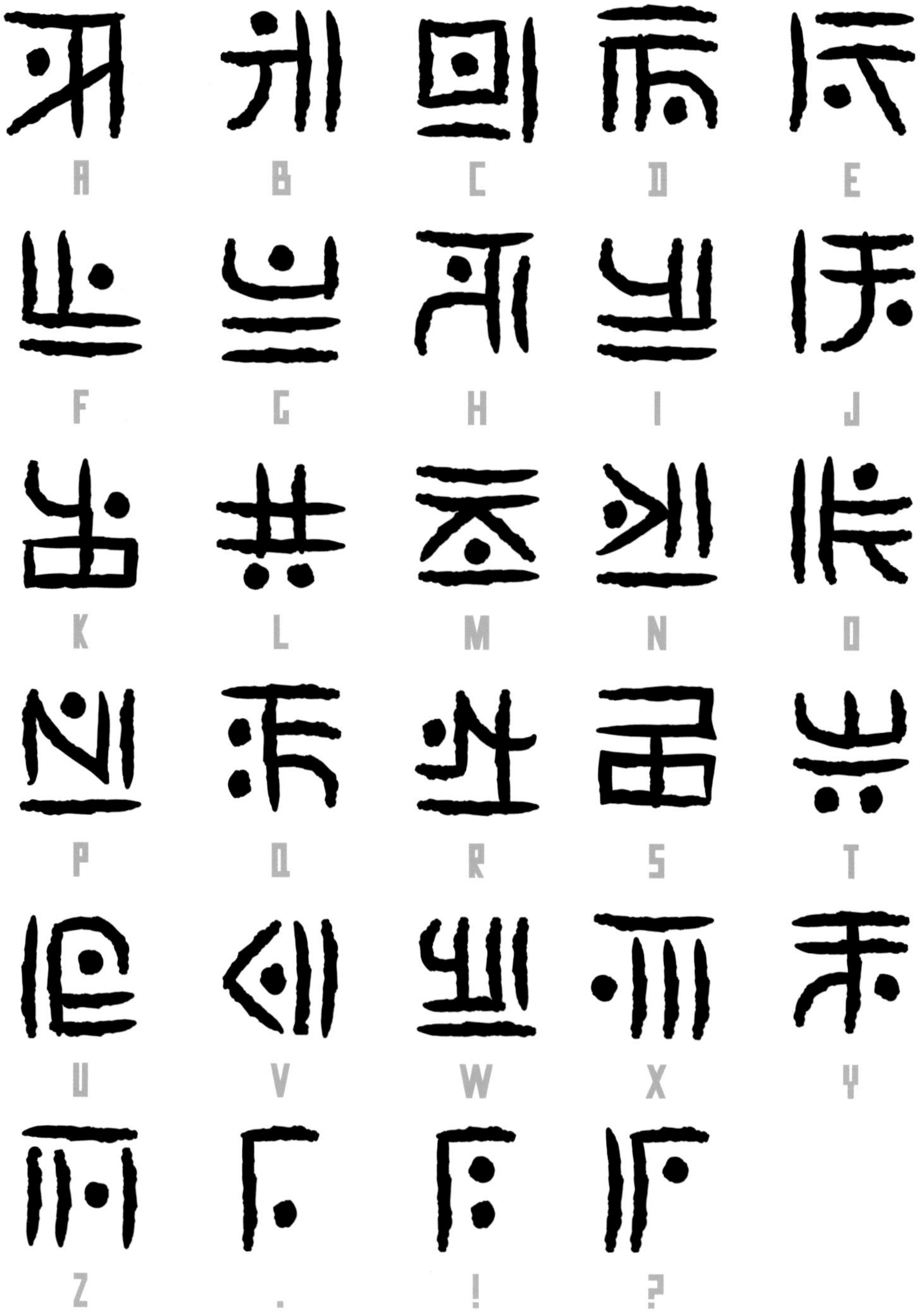

Using a custom brush in Adobe Illustrator, I drew out a clean, final version of the font with a uniform weight. The little bit of texture in the line weight gives the font some character. Letterforms alone don't make a font, and I still needed to add some punctuation. My thinking was that an alien or future language would be streamlined and wouldn't have the contractions we are used to in contemporary English, so I got rid of apostrophes and kept basic punctuation marks. Question mark, exclamation point, period - what more do you need?! Designing and making the letters is one thing, but turning them into a working font with proper kerning and other meticulous settings is another matter entirely. I called on a fellow native Rhode Islander, Nate Piekos of Blambot Studios, to help bring this over the finish line. Nate has designed some of the best fonts around, so I knew he could turn this pile of letters into a beautiful working font, one that I was able to use in thirty issues of *Paper Girls*. I'm grateful for his hard work.

A.N.D.G. Cards

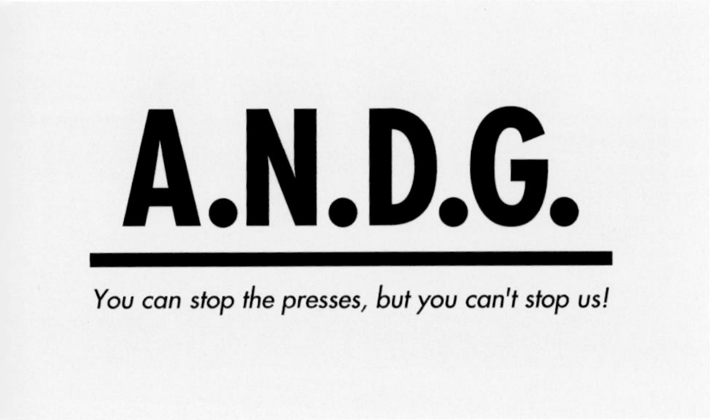

The membership card for the American Newspaper Delivery Guild (A.N.D.G.) was a mail-in offer from the back of the single-issue comics. Using the old-fashioned delivery method of the post office, motivated readers could mail away for these exclusive membership cards. My own experience as a kid with this sort of club was the shabby clown that would come on the air with other child actors to promote the regional TV station's "kids club" between cartoons. The station mailed you a personalized membership card if you sent them the self-addressed stamped envelope. To replicate that concept and others like it, I designed a throwback to those old '80s card layouts and fit it to our little club. It's a deliberate nostalgia move, which was elevated by Cliff's wonderful art for mascot Petey Roy.

The hard labor of filling out, laminating, and mailing all the cards fell to Brian's poor family. (I understand he's a bit of a tyrant.) So a big thanks for all their efforts in helping build the A.N.D.G. community. I always encourage members to bring their cards to cons and book store signings. Any time I travel to a comic convention, I make sure to pack my A.N.D.G. card in the hopes of meeting other members.

Reference!

Cliff and I had several talks about what kinds of '80s references we wanted to pull from visually and what we wanted to ignore. Teen girl magazines of that era were a particular focus. *YM* and *Sassy* were the big two I started gathering for reference files, and after some eBay digging, I immersed myself in their visual language: fonts, logos, page layouts, cover designs, product ads, music and film. I was looking to convey the feel of that time in my design of the book overall and the logo in particular.

We discussed some iconic magazines, and both *Interview* and *Sassy* had wonderful brush logos. These were a great reference point for the kind of textured, dry brush feel I wanted to evoke.

Having a piece of cover art is always an enormous help in designing a logo because it can set the tone of the book and better inform the design direction. Cliff sent an early sketch of the teaser image we planned to announce the series with at Image Expo in 2015. An amazingly atmospheric piece of art, it placed a lot of emphasis on the creators, a bike handlebar, and the logo. The logo itself needed to hold its own as a design, it needed to be equally as evocative as the art, and it needed to have a similar feel to the art. The end result ended up a perfect example of how a good logo can make an impact, help set the tone, and generate interest from the readers.

Andy Warhol's
Interview

Interview

Sassy

Digital Sketches

Swimming in all this reference, the next step was to go diving for fonts. Usually I dig through my own font archives, and if needed I go shopping for new fonts if the project budget allows. My plan for this project was to find several promising fonts to use as baseline reference. Then I would digitally sketch the "Paper Girls" logo by manipulating the letterforms of different fonts. Finally, I would hand letter each version of the logo (traditionally, on paper) over these digital sketches.

In the sketches, I stayed with the brush theme and played around with different letterforms and approaches to the logo. My goal was to get a feel for the sketches that best communicated the tone of the book. How obviously retro should it look? Too much nostalgia can steer the design into parody, so finding that balance is important. I was trying to create something that looked like it could be from the 1980s, and yet was classic enough to feel contemporary to 2010s, and also could evoke something of the future, all while being its own unique design.

Caligraphy Brushes

Once we decided which of the sketches was the best option, I started prepping to ink. I fit six copies of the digital logo sketch onto a page and printed out six large copies. I usually print the sketches in a light blue color and treat them like a digital "pencil" sketch that I can ink over. I used a few different brushes to ink the thirty-six versions of the logo. There had to be a certain level of dry brush and texture to the inks to get the look I was going for, and I gave myself thirty-six chances to find something just right. I didn't worry about getting any one version of the logo perfect since I was going to cobble the final logo together from the best versions of the inks. The P and G are particularly interchangeable but also very unique and important to the whole design. I wanted to try a variety of takes so I could mix and match for the best complete design.

I inked all the logos first and then followed up with the number sets. Since the number set was printed physically smaller, I stuck to just one brush for the inks. I wanted to stay in rhythm while inking the smaller numbers to try and achieve a better consistency. Finding the best option of each number was easier than all the mix and match possibilities of the logo. I singled out any version that looked good in the inks and then ran a side by side comparison of everything on my computer screen after it was all scanned.

Paper Girls

Paper Girls

Paper Girls

Digital finish

After I picked out the different pieces I liked in the inks, I scanned the inked pages and isolated all the letters and numbers I wanted to use and cleaned them up in Adobe Photoshop. Then I switched over to Adobe Illustrator to convert the scanned inks into vector art. The vectors allowed me to scale and manipulate the letterforms as I built out new versions of the logo. I pulled about a dozen options for the logo from the inked scans and I started mixing different combinations to build out the next stage of the designs. These three logos were the final result of all the planning, research, sketching, inking, scanning, manipulating, tinkering, and deliberation that preceded them.

The final version mixes my favorite versions of the letterforms into a cohesive whole. The final logo captures that '80s brush feel I was chasing while also standing as a modern design. This logo ended up being the first of a small run of successful logos working in a similar style. I had used this method before but the results really seemed to resonate with the Paper Girls logo.

Paper Girls

0123456789

CREATORS

BRIAN K. VAUGHAN
Activities: Theater, Sci-Fi Book Club, Power of the Pen
Worst Subject: Math, P.E. (tie)
Halloween Costume: Homemade Spider-Man Symbiote Suit

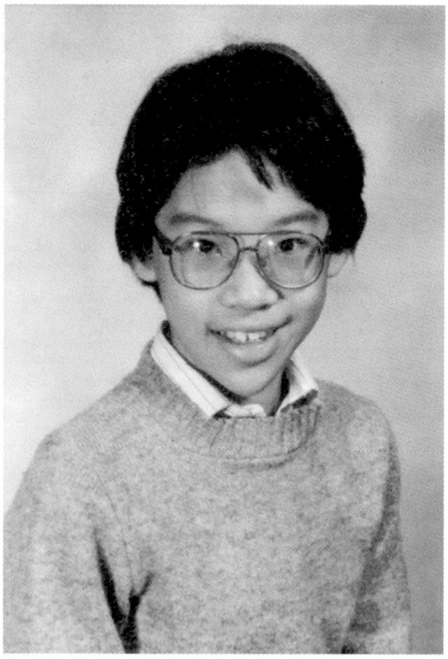

CLIFF CHIANG
Homeroom: Miss Benson
Activities: Chorus, Ski Club, French Cultural Society, Art Club
Favorite NES games: *Contra, Double Dribble, Metal Gear*

MATT WILSON
Homeroom: Miss Pearce
Activities: Basketball, Art Club, Taekwondo, skateboarding
Favorite toys: Battle Beasts, M.A.S.K., The Centurions, G.I. Joe, TMNT

JARED K. FLETCHER
Homeroom: Mr. Chandler
Activities: Sailing, Art Club, Wrestling, talking too much
Favorite Lego set: Space Monorail Transport System 6990